THE WITCH WHO SAW A MURDER

PIXIE POINT BAY BOOK 8

EMMA BELMONT

EMMA ONLINE

Emma loves hearing from her readers!

You can contact her at the links below.

Website: emmabelmont.com

Newsletter: emmabelmont.com/newsletter

Thanks!

1

Maris carried the blanket, Bear carried the basket, and Cookie brought the thermoses. Though the Towne Plaza was enormous, it was starting to look like the beach in summer, with colorful ground coverings and coolers everywhere.

"Goodness," Maris said. "I didn't realize Pixie Point Bay Picnic Day was going to be so popular."

"They always are," Cookie said, smiling and looking around. Her bright floral dress matched the surroundings perfectly. "I haven't been to one of these in years."

It wasn't often that Ruth "Cookie" Calderon came to town at all. The B&B's chef always said that she preferred home—particularly her kitchen and garden—to just about anywhere.

Picnic Day, however, was an exception.

"How about here?" Maris asked her companions. She came to a stop and surveyed the neatly trimmed patch of grass about midway to the Oriental gazebo.

"Fine by me," the diminutive chef said, looking at her, and then up at Bear.

Their outsized handyman grinned at her. "Looks good."

He easily stood two heads above them and carried the heavily laden picnic basket as though it was a lunchbox. His neatly trimmed beard didn't hide his smile. Nor did his bib overalls hide a burgeoning paunch at the midriff.

"Great," Maris said, and unfurled the checkered blanket.

"Is that the new pizzeria?" Cookie asked, looking in its direction.

Located in a building that was even narrower than the medical clinic, wedged between Castaways and Superior Hardware, was the newest establishment in town: Pizza del Popolo.

Maris glanced in that direction as she

continued to spread out the blanket. "That's the one," she confirmed.

Cookie nodded. "It's about time."

Bear sniffed the air. "I can smell it." He arched his heavy brows. "It smells good."

Satisfied with the blanket, Maris gazed in the pizzeria's direction. "I'm happy to say it tastes good too." Bear swiveled his head back to her. "He's having his soft opening this week, and I was invited for a sample." She grinned at him. "It's good to be the owner of the Pixie Point Bay Lighthouse and B&B."

Not only was it her job to ensure the comfort of her guests, but they often asked for restaurant recommendations. She regularly sampled new menu offerings, even at places she'd eaten many times.

"Shall we have a seat?" Cookie said. As she sat down on the blanket, Bear placed the basket next to her. "Thank you, Bear."

Maris paused to scan the area. "Oh, there he is," she said, and waved.

Mac saw her, waved back, and headed their way. She watched him stride over. It always pleased her to see him dressed in something other than his uniform. Six feet tall and athletically built, Sheriff McKenna of Medio

County had the kind of rugged good looks that made hearts flutter. His gray eyes and matching salt and pepper hair only added to his charm.

She held out her hands to him as he approached. He took them and leaned in for a quick peck on the cheek.

"I'm glad you could make it," Maris said.

"I wouldn't have missed it," he replied before pulling away and looking down at her. "You look lovely."

She'd made sure to wear the most flattering skirt and blouse that she owned, and had taken extra time with her hair. Despite having aimed for exactly that compliment, heat rose to her cheeks. "Thank you."

Mac nodded to the chef. "Cookie. It's good to see you."

Cookie had opened the basket, but paused, smiling as she shielded her eyes from the sun. "Nice to see you too, Sheriff."

He reached across Maris and offered his hand to Bear. "Good morning, Bear. How's it going?"

"Very well, Mac," he said, shaking the sheriff's hand. "And you?"

Mac grinned at him, and then at Maris. "Never better."

Bear gave him a little nod as he nimbly descended into a cross-legged position, facing Cookie. Not as light as the chef nor as young as their handyman, Maris took her time getting to the ground, with a helping hand from Mac. Since arriving back in Pixie Point Bay she felt more healthy than she had in decades. With her weight steadily if slowly dropping, she expected that her cholesterol would be getting to a good range too. But it didn't mean she was any more limber. When she finally sat down, Mac joined her, and Cookie started to unpack the basket.

"Maris, would you pour the tea please?" She handed her the plastic mugs, and then a thermos.

"My pleasure," Maris said. She'd just been unscrewing the plastic top when a voice assailed her from behind.

"Maris," he said. "*Ciao, Bella!*"

Before she turned her head, she had to smile. "Massimo," she said, seeing him approach. "Oh!" she exclaimed. He was barreling toward them with a stack of pizza boxes in his arms.

In his early fifties, the owner of the new pizzeria wasn't particularly a big man but he'd impressed Maris as 'solid.' The hint of a beard at the jaw line and his short mustache were only flecked with gray. But his hair—shaved close at the sides and combed back on top—was a lustrous chestnut brown. The short haircut emphasized the one cauliflower ear, and Maris had previously noticed his bent nose.

As he reached the blanket, he quickly crouched and set down the pizzas. Kneeling next to her, he leaned closer for an air kiss on one cheek, then the other.

"How wonderful to see you," he said. Without waiting for introductions, he extended a hand to Cookie. "I am Massimo Cuore, but please call me Max."

She smiled at him as they shook. "Cookie Calderon."

He paused, his mouth open in shock as he glanced at Maris. "The chef?" Maris smiled and nodded. He took Cookie's hand in both of his and gave her a little bow. "It is an honor to finally meet you. I have heard about you...*everywhere.*"

"Oh, well," Cookie said, her face flushing

pink. "That's very kind." She glanced down at their hands, looking more flustered than Maris had ever seen the older woman.

"Oh, pardon!" he said, and let her hand go. "I am in disbelief that I am actually meeting you."

When the diminutive chef seemed lost for words, Maris said, "And this is Sheriff Daniel McKenna."

Mac shook the chef's hand. "We've actually already met," the sheriff said. "Good to see you."

"You've met?" Maris asked.

Max nodded. "At the County Recorders office." He grinned at Mac. "I was lost but luckily the sheriff found me."

It was no wonder that the crows feet at the corners of Max's dark eyes were deep because, as always, his smile was enormous. As usual he wore a traditional white chef's shirt, but modified with a stripe of bright green running down one side of his chest, and a stripe of red down the other.

"And may I introduce Bear Orsino." She gestured to the big man. "The world's most accomplished handyman."

Max thrust his hand forward, peering

into Bear's face. "Orsino? From the old country?"

Bear took the man's hand. "Abruzzo. My grandfather."

Max slapped his other hand over Bear's enormous one and shook it vigorously. "Ho, *compagno!*" he exclaimed, beaming. "My family too. Maybe near Matelica?"

Bear shook his head but grinned. "Pioraco."

"Oh, the mountains!" He regarded the young man. "Fitting. Very fitting."

"Massimo," Maris said. "Would you–"

"Please call me Max," he said, putting on a hurt look. "We are friends, are we not?"

Maris laughed a little. "Max," she started again, "would you like to join us?"

He put a hand over his heart as he sat back on his heels. "I am honored. Truly." Then he reached to the boxes of pizza, took one, and handed it to her. "But I am on my tour of the plaza. Free pizza for everyone."

Maris cocked her head back as she accepted it. "Free pizza?"

Cookie added, "For everyone?" She gazed around at the plaza.

"Yes," he said, nodding. Then he stood.

"So I best go on my way." He took them all in with a fond look. "It was a pleasure to meet you."

Maris opened the box top and took a peek. The beautiful smell of the tomato sauce and fresh crust immediately wafted up.

"A seafood pizza?" she said, as Max bent and picked up the rest of the boxes.

He grinned down at her. "When in Roma, eh?" Then he was off, heading toward the next blanket. "*Ciao, amici!*"

"Look at that," Cookie said, gazing down into the box with awe in her voice. "Are those scallops?"

"And baby shrimp and crab meat," Mac said nodding.

"I can smell the garlic," Bear said.

Maris was about to set the box down so they could all take a slice, but then she remembered the basket. Cookie had spent the morning getting their picnic ready.

When the chef noticed her gaze, she closed and patted its wicker top. "It'll keep." Then she eyed the pizza. "Let's give this a try."

Maris quickly set the box down and they each took a slice. Bear folded his piece and was the first to take a bite. "Mmm hmm," he murmured.

Maris had already sampled Max's triple mushroom pizza earlier in the week. But as she took her first bite, she knew immediately that this was completely different. He'd changed the tomato sauce to compliment the seafood—just a tad on the zesty side.

Mac nodded as he chewed. He gave Maris the thumbs up sign.

Cookie was next. As the chef sampled her slice, Maris saw the gears turning behind the dark and glittering eyes. She covered her mouth as she said, "Oh, that is good." She looked down at her slice, analyzing it. "Asiago instead of Parmesan. Very nice choice. It's–"

"Pig!" said a woman's shrill voice. "Chauvinist pig!"

Not ten yards away, a woman was shaking her fist at someone.

"Who is that?" Maris asked. She didn't recognize either of them.

"Rudy Schmid," Bear said.

"The owner of Superior Hardware," Cookie said, glaring at him with distaste. She peered at the pair a while longer before returning to her pizza. "I don't know the woman."

The tall man standing in front of her, on what was presumably his blanket, had his arms folded over his chest and was laughing. He shook his head and said something Maris couldn't make out. The woman was so angry that she was shaking.

Maris looked back at Bear and Cookie, who were eating their pizza, making her frown. "Wait a minute," she said, reluctantly setting her slice down, just as Mac did. "That woman just called him a pig, and is obviously livid. Am I the only one bothered about it?"

Bear shrugged. "It's Rudy." He took another bite.

Cookie nodded. "He is a pig."

Maris stared at her. "What?"

"That's it!" the woman screamed. As Maris watched, she spun on her heel, stalked off—and tripped.

"Oh no," Maris said, as the angry woman went down in a pile. Thank goodness they were on grass. She must have tripped on someone's blanket.

Mac shot to his feet but a young man nearby went over to help her up. But when he

bent over her, he crouched down. His pan-
icked face, as he scanned the plaza, said
everything.

"Ambulance," he yelled. "Someone get an
ambulance!"

2

Maris jumped to her feet and hurried over with Mac, as did Jill Maxwell, the nurse practitioner of the medical clinic. Mac already had his phone out and was calling emergency dispatch.

"Joy?" Jill said, dropping to her knees beside the woman. "Joy, can you hear me?" But the poor woman had fallen face down, head turned to the side, and wasn't moving. Jill bent low to look into her face. "Joy, it's Jill, can you hear me?"

The nurse quickly removed a small vinyl pouch with a red cross on it from her back pocket. As she took out a pair of gloves from it and snapped them on, she said to Mac, "Her eyes are open but she's not responsive."

She bent back down, close to Joy's face. From where Maris stood behind Jill, she could see that, although the woman's eyes were open, they were drooping and her entire face was slack.

"Joy!" Minako Page exclaimed, coming up behind them. She stopped beside Maris, her hand flying to her mouth. "Oh no."

"Ambulance is on the way," Mac said, crouching down on Joy's other side.

"I'm going to touch your shoulders, Joy," Jill said to her, laying her hands on them. "Can you feel this?" Again there was no response. She glanced at Mac. "I'd rather not move her, in case of spinal or head injury." She stared at Joy's back. "She's not breathing."

Maris felt a sudden sinking feeling in her stomach. Minako clutched her arm.

"Joy, I'm going to check your airway," Jill said, using her fingers to open the woman's mouth. She tilted her head, and lowered the jaw. "It's clear."

Maris realized that the entire plaza had gone still, several people standing, and all eyes on Jill. Minako's husband Alfred had appeared next to her. "Is she injured?"

"No choice," Jill said to Mac. "I need to turn her over."

Moving in tandem, as though their steady movements had been drilled into them, Jill moved Joy's arms upward, and Mac crossed her legs at the ankle.

"On three," Jill said, as she placed her hand alongside Joy's jaw. "One." Mac grasped Joy's pants at the hip. "Two." Jill used her other hand to grasp Joy's shoulder. Mac placed a stabilizing hand against her back. "Three."

As though Joy was as light as a child, the sheriff and nurse rolled her smoothly over. Jill snatched something else from her vinyl pouch. It was a clear plastic mask labelled "CPR MASK" with a small circular respirator in the center. Deftly, Jill looped the elastic bands around Joy's ears. She tilted her head back, lowered her head to Joy's, and blew into the respirator. Maris saw Joy's chest rise, and then fall. Mac put gloved fingers to Joy's neck. Maris had no idea when he'd put on the gloves. Jill gave Joy another rescue breath, watched her chest rise, fall, and then stay still.

"Come on," the nurse muttered. "Come on." She gave Joy another breath.

"No pulse," Mac said. He immediately bent over Joy's chest, placed one hand over another in the middle of it, and pushed.

Maris turned to the Pages whose faces had gone white. She stood in front of them, blocking their view. "Where is your blanket?"

Minako blinked at her. "What?"

Maris looked at Alfred. "Take Minako back to your blanket and sit down." Taller than her, Alfred was still staring at Joy over Maris's head. She put a hand on his arm. "Alfred, take Minako back to your blanket."

As though he'd finally heard her, he quickly nodded. "Right." He grasped his wife by the shoulders, and turned her around. "Let's go."

A siren sounded in the distance, rapidly growing closer. When she turned back to Mac and Jill, they were still performing CPR, their faces determined but grim. Joy's eyes, the lids still half closed, were staring up into the sun.

The ambulance rolled into view, parked at the sidewalk, and the three person EMT crew jumped out. They ran over, kits in hand.

"Stretcher," Jill gasped between breaths. Mac was continuing chest compressions. More people in the plaza were standing, but no one approached.

Two of the EMTs exchanged a quick look and ran back to the ambulance, while the other dashed over, set down his kit, and felt for a pulse. Seemingly in seconds, the other two were back with the metal gurney. Again, as though they had all rehearsed, they quickly lifted the limp woman to the stretcher. Jill and Mac both resumed CPR as the EMTs rolled the gurney. Maris lost sight of them as they entered the back of the ambulance, bringing the stretcher with them. One got out and went to the driver's seat. The engine started up. Mac jumped down from the back, and helped Jill do the same. When he closed the door and thumped on it twice, the siren flared up again and the ambulance took off.

For a few moments, the sheriff and nurse exchanged words. Then they trotted over to Alfred and Minako. Maris followed behind. Although Alfred stood, Minako remained sitting.

"Is she all right?" he asked.

"What happened to her?" Minako said.

Jill wasn't looking at them though. She was looking at their picnic. On the blanket were two Japanese bento boxes, which presumably belonged to the Pages, and an unopened box of pizza. But Jill was pointing to the other food. "Is that what Joy was eating?"

Minako stared at the bag of tortilla chips, an unlabelled jar of salsa, and a half-eaten tuna salad sandwich.

"Yes," Alfred said.

"That was her lunch," Minako added.

Jill looked from one to the other of them. "Have either of you had any of her food?"

Though still sitting on her knees, Minako inched away from it. "No," she said, her voice trembling. "We..."

"Brought our own," Alfred said.

As Jill carefully removed her gloves, and tossed them to the blanket, Mac stepped forward. "I'm going to need you to go with Jill to the medical clinic. She's going to ask you some questions." He surveyed the blanket. "You're going to have to leave everything. Forensics is on the way to collect it."

"Forensics?" Alfred said, helping his wife up.

"Why does forensics need our food?" Minako said.

Jill helped her to stand as well, taking her by the elbow. "I hope I'm wrong, but Joy may be suffering from some type of neurotoxin poisoning. It could have come from the food."

"Oh no," Minako said. "Will she be all right?"

Jill had already started leading them to the clinic. "I'll call the emergency room in Cheeseman Village as soon as we're through."

As the threesome made their way across the grass, muffled conversations started up in their trail.

Maris leaned close to Mac. "How is Joy?"

He shook his head, took his gloves off inside out, and tossed them next to Jill's. "She's dead," he said quietly.

3

As the forensics crew bagged and tagged everything, including the Page's blanket, they chatted with Mac as Maris stood by. Senior Investigator Lucille Trahan and her young assistant, Sefina Kealoha, were dressed in the usual white biohazard suits, masks, and gloves. But with the thought of a neurotoxin possibly being present, the outfits seemed particularly apt.

"If I was to hazard a guess," Lucille was saying, as she put the bagged sandwich in a plastic box, "I'd say botulinum toxin."

"Really," Mac said, notepad in hand, now entirely in sheriff mode. "I thought that took days."

The heavyset older woman, shrugged.

"It'd depend on the dose. It can be as little as a few hours."

Sefina brought over the chips and salsa and deposited them in the box. Just then, Max came up beside Maris. She glanced at his worried face and saw him staring at the pizza box, which had been placed in a large plastic bag.

"Would any of these foods have been particularly suspect?" the sheriff asked.

Lucille pointed at the sandwich. "My bet would be on the tuna. *Clostridium botulinum* loves seafood."

Max gasped a little. "My pizza today was seafood."

Sefina looked up at him. "Do you used canned fish?"

Max shook his head vigorously. "Never. Only fresh from the pier and Captain Duff."

The young woman's dark eyes smiled at him. "Then it wasn't the pizza."

Lucille nodded. "The bacteria is virtually everywhere around us, but it thrives in low oxygen where it produces the toxin that actually kills people. Just one microgram is lethal." She gazed from Max to Maris and finally the sheriff. "That's one-millionth of a gram."

"Whoa," Maris said.

"*Davvero?*" Max whispered. "Really?"

"Whatever is carrying it," Lucille said to Mac, "that was good thinking to stop the other people here from eating."

He nodded at the medical clinic. "We can thank Jill Maxwell for that. She's with the Pages now, making sure they're all right."

Maris glanced around the plaza. About half of the picnickers had left. Bear and Cookie were still on their blanket, quietly having the meal that Cookie had prepared. Since they'd all come in one car, they were waiting for her. But as her gaze swept the rest of the plaza, she noticed Rudy Schmid, the owner of Superior Hardware, and a woman his age with him.

"The owner of the hardware store and Joy had just had an argument," Maris reminded Mac. "I thought she was so angry that she was shaking. But now I'm thinking it might have been the result of the botulism."

As Mac followed her gaze, his face soured. "I've dealt with Mr. Schmid before.

But he's within his rights to refuse service to whoever he wants."

"Refuse service?" Maris asked, her brows knitting together. "Like to Joy? You think that's why she was mad?"

"I expect so," Mac said, putting away the notebook. "He refuses service to all women. I'm pretty sure that he's a misogynist."

Maris recalled what Cookie had said. "I see," she muttered. "But who is that woman with him?"

"Heather Schmid," the Italian chef answered. "I ran into her on the sidewalk, quite literally."

"His wife," Mac added and then sighed. "I'm going to have a word with him."

Jill was returning with Alfred and Minako and Mac paused. As they approached, he gave them a smile. "Everything good, I hope?"

"Completely asymptomatic," Jill answered. "In fact, they're in excellent health."

"Good," the sheriff said, turning to them. "I'll find you at your store. I assume you're going back there."

They'd both been staring at the forensics

team, folding up the blanket. "Uh, yes," Alfred finally said.

"The store is open," Minako told the sheriff.

"Fine," Mac said. "I'll see you there later." He indicated the Schmids. "I'll be talking with Mr. Schmid first."

When the sheriff had left, Alfred put his arm around Minako's shoulders, but addressed Maris. "Jill called the hospital in Cheeseman Village. Joy was pronounced dead on arrival."

Maris gave them both a pained looked. "I'm so sorry."

Max clutched his hands to his chest. "No, *mi amici.* So terrible." He watched as the forensics team began to pack up. "How fragile life is." He looked back to Minako and Alfred. "Please call on me if there is anything I can do."

ALTHOUGH MAX DEPARTED, Maris stayed with the Pages. As though they were trying to hold on to the last of their friend, they silently watched the forensics team put away their unused evidence bags. In the background, however, Maris couldn't help but overhear Mac and Rudy Schmid only several feet behind her.

"Yeah, I told her to leave," Rudy was saying. "She had no business shopping for a plumber's wrench. I doubt she could even lift one."

"What time was this?" Mac said.

"Right at opening," the owner replied. "Seven this morning."

There was a pause, probably as the sheriff made a note. "And why did she have no business shopping for a plumber's wrench?"

Rudy made a rude and dismissive sound. "Because those are for plumbers."

"Would you sell one to me?" Mac asked.

"Why, you do your own plumbing?" Rudy retorted.

Maris's brows drew together and she nearly turned around to look. It wasn't often people took that tone with the sheriff.

"It's none of your business what I'd do with a wrench," Mac said calmly. "Now, would you sell one to me?"

There was an uncomfortable pause that

made Maris smirk. Finally, Rudy said, "Sure. Why not. It's your money to waste."

"So you asked Ms. Castro to leave the premises," the sheriff said. "What happened then?"

Rudy snorted. "She pitched a little hissy fit and left."

For a few moments, there was silence. The forensics teams had finished packing up and had begun to take the materials they'd collected to the van.

"I can't believe this," Minako whispered.

"She was so full of life," Alfred agreed. Together, they heaved a heavy sigh.

The two forensics investigators returned for their tool boxes. They picked them up and Sefina took hers to the van, while Lucille went over to Mac. As the Pages turned to watch her, so did Maris.

"That's it for us, Sheriff," the Senior Investigator said. "If there's nothing else you need, we'll head back to the lab."

Mac nodded to her. "Thank you, Lucille. I'll be in touch."

Alfred looked down at his wife. He took a handkerchief from his pocket and gave it to her. "I guess we'd better get back..."

She nodded, and wiped her eyes. "...to the store."

He tried to give Maris a smile, not quite succeeding. "Thanks for your help, Maris."

Minako nodded as she sniffed. "Yes, thank you."

Maris smiled and patted her lightly on the back. "I haven't done a thing, but I'll check on you both later."

As they made their way back across the plaza, Mac had apparently finished with Rudy and his wife, and joined the Pages as they headed to their store.

Rudy and his wife sat back down on their blanket. Maris could see that Max had given them a pizza, but the box looked unopened. Instead, it looked like they were having fried chicken, mashed potatoes and rolls. As she turned away from them, Maris realized she hadn't had lunch but now she'd lost her appetite.

4

Maris arrived back at the blanket to find Max standing with Bear and Cookie. The blanket had been folded, and lay neatly on top of the picnic basket, with the pizza box on top. The Italian chef's gaze darted from the medical clinic to Inklings and then the pizzeria, and then back to the medical clinic.

"The grand opening is just days away now," he was saying to Cookie. He tugged nervously on his cauliflower ear. "To have my food associated with a deadly event is a disaster."

Maris joined them. "The forensics team is going to sort this out quickly," she assured him. "It's most certainly a public health risk."

"Of course, of course," he said, though he sounded far from convinced.

"Max," Cookie said, "your food had nothing to do with that poor woman's death. We all had your wonderful pizza—and enjoyed it I might add—and there's not a single sign that anyone is feeling poorly."

Bear pointed down at the closed pizza box. "We saved you a piece, Maris."

She smiled at him. "Thank you, Bear. I'll have it later. For the moment, I seem to have lost my appetite."

Max threw his hands in the air. "This is exactly what I am talking about. Even if it is not my food, now everyone is a bit suspicious of everything. Everyone will remember what happened here today. Is anyone going to come to a restaurant opening here?"

"Of course they will," Maris assured him. "I know I'm looking forward to it."

Max smiled at her, tilting his head. "Ah *Bella*, of course you would say this. We are friends."

Cookie grinned at him. "Well we're not, and I am most definitely looking forward to Pizza del Popolo's grand opening."

Bear nodded. "Me too."

Max had to laugh a little, easing the tension lines in his forehead. He took them all in with a smile. "Ah *mi amici*, my friends. Truly, you lift my heart."

"We'll do more than that," Maris declared. "I'm happy to help you in any way that I can. Just say the word."

"Same here," Cookie said. "Your wonderful food deserves the best grand opening that can be. I'm with Maris. If there's anything that I can do to help, please call."

Bear grinned a little. "Me too."

Max beamed at them and extended his arms. "With such support, how can I fail?"

5

Late afternoon sun poured into the optics house as Maris and Bear climbed the last steps up to it. For a big man, Maris was astonished at how easily he seemed to trot up the spiral staircase, bouncing from one step to the next. Not wanting to fall behind, she'd pushed herself to do the same, and was panting hard for her effort. She was excited to learn about maintaining the lighthouse, but that didn't translate to suddenly being in shape—or twenty years younger.

"Phew!" she exhaled as she came to a stop on the metal platform. "I think you must have..." She took in a deep breath. "...set a new speed record." She blew it out as she wiped a trickle of sweat from her forehead.

"It's got to be a new..." She paused for a gulp of air. "...personal best for me."

"You can go slower," he said. "I don't mind waiting."

"Bear," she said smiling, as she tried to get her breathing under control, "I don't imagine there's anything you'd mind."

He lightly combed his fingers through his beard, apparently thinking. Finally he nodded. "Not much."

Though Bear turned to the fresnel lens, Maris paused for a moment to take in the view. The brilliant sunlight twinkled from the water below, as though each wave held its own star. A small boat skimmed through them, its billowed sail puffing out in front. The deepening blue hues of the crystal clear water stretched to the horizon, where bands of clouds streamed right and left. She could watch the changing sky and water for hours, but she'd come here with Bear for a job.

As Maris turned to face him, she said, "Where do you want to start?"

"At the bottom," he replied. He pointed to the metal grate on which they stood. "All of the wrought iron needs to have the paint stripped and any rust removed. Then it can be repainted."

"How often is it needed?" she asked, crouching down when Bear did.

He ran his fingers over the diamond pattern of the grating. "When it starts to peel or flake off." He looked at his fingertips, which were clean. "If it's just a little bit, then sometimes I only redo that spot." He stood and touched the frame around one of the optics house's many windows. "These too. All of the metal. You can't let it rust."

Maris stood and nodded. "All right. No rust on the metal. Repaint when it starts to flake."

"Yes," Bear said.

She regarded the fresnel lens, and the metal that held all the pieces of glass in their complex arrangement. "What about this metal?"

Bear shook his head. "It's stainless steel. You never have to touch it, so you shouldn't."

Maris blinked. "Oh. I had no idea." Though she'd often patted the fresnel lens's glass base, she couldn't recall if she'd ever touched the steel.

He pointed below it to the pedestal. "Inside are the ball bearings and the motor. Both have to be greased from time to time because they aren't sealed. The access panel is in the back."

"Access panel?" she said, dumbfounded. She'd never seen such a thing.

Bear walked around the lens to its other side. "Here."

Maris followed him and stared down at the curving metal door, painted the same black as the floor and window frames. A small padlock hung from the closed latch.

"Good grief," she said, staring at it. "I've never noticed it." She glanced outside to the view of the attached B&B and the lands beyond. "I guess I'm always looking out."

"That's mostly why people come up here," he agreed.

Maris shook her head. "Still, I can't believe I missed it." She was starting to see the Old Girl in a completely new light.

"There's an ambient light sensor outside that I check once a month," Bear said, pointing back to the front of the optics house. "And we also have a backup generator down below that I run once a month, but I've never seen us lose electricity."

The sensor was what triggered the beam to come on when the light was low enough. She'd never wondered where it was located. The backup generator she had seen though.

"Is that the red engine-looking thing on the first floor?" she asked.

"Yes," he said.

Her head was starting to swim with all the new information. "And we haven't even got to the glass yet."

"We're there now," he said. He wiped a thick index finger on one of the panes. It left a clean trail in the light haze on the glass. "Inside and out, the storm panes have to be cleaned regularly. Otherwise the beam can't go as far as it possibly can."

Maris nodded. "That makes sense."

"These should be cleaned tomorrow," he said. He turned to the enormous egg-shaped glass and stainless steel structure. "The fresnel lens doesn't need as much cleaning, but it's for the same reason."

Maris regarded it. "To throw out as much light as possible." It's myriad pieces of glass were also all etched with fine concentric circles. "How do you clean it?"

"With a soft microfiber cloth," Bear said,

"nothing more." He glanced down at himself. "I'd show you now, but I'm not dressed for it."

She scowled at him. "Not dressed for it?"

He quickly shook his head. "No belt buckles, or watches, or jewelry when touching the lens. Never."

"Oh wow," she muttered. "Of course. You don't want to accidentally scratch it."

Bear nodded and eyed the horizon. "I can show you how to clean it tomorrow."

As the sun slowly descended in the western sky, evening was approaching. Maris knew that Bear liked to be home before dark.

"That sounds good," she said. As they made their way back to the stairs, she said, "Do you get everything you need at Superior Hardware?"

He waited at the door that led to the spiral staircase and stood aside. "Yes," he said.

She paused before proceeding through. "So you've known Rudy Schmid for some time?"

As Maris watched, she saw Bear do something she'd never seen before—he frowned. "He's not a very nice man."

From anyone else, it might have described someone who took money from the tip jar. From Bear, it was a condemnation.

The big man shrugged. "It's the only hardware store in town."

"Right," Maris said, preceding him and then starting down. "Right."

6

If the wine and cheese had a theme, Maris decided that tonight's would be contrast. As usual, she took the large cheeseboard and all of its ingredients to the sideboard in the dining room where she would assemble it. Occasionally a guest would wander in early, get a preview taste, or simply watch her work. It was a system she'd stumbled upon years ago in her hotel work. That particular Wine Down had been more relaxed, chatty, and convivial than any other that had preceded it. She'd stuck with the winning recipe ever since.

First, of course, she opened tonight's local wines: a Riesling from Crown Winery and a port from Alegra. While the white varietal of German origin was dry and crisp, the port's sweetness was thick bodied. That was the first contrast. She placed them on the dining room table along with enough glasses for all of her guests to sample each.

The fresh cheeses from the Cheeseman Village Dairy complimented the wines: the pungent and crumbly bleu cheese was the perfect foil for the port, while the sweet and tangy ricotta cheese paired wonderfully with the Riesling.

As she sliced a little of the cheese and arranged it on the cheeseboard, her mind wandered back to the picnic.

"Contrast again," she said lowly.

In the span of a few seconds, the pleasant meal had turned deadly. They'd gone from being pleasantly assailed by Max and his free pizza, to an argument in their midst, and then a death. Though the two latter events seemed related, Maris had to wonder. From what the forensics investigator had said, the earliest symptoms of botulinum toxin would take three hours to surface. Joy must have eaten something before the argument.

"Am I early?" a woman's voice asked from the doorway.

Maris turned to see Patricia Linn-Baker at

the dining room entrance and smiled at the large woman. "There's no such thing when it comes to wine and cheese."

As she entered the room, her green eyes went immediately to the cheeseboard. "Oh, how lovely."

Maris had recognized not only her guest's name but also her face. The renowned food critic had columns in newspapers and magazines all over the country. Formerly of Michelin, she was independent now.

"Can I pour you some port or a dry Riesling?" Maris said, setting aside the cheese knife and using a dish towel to wipe her hands.

"Mmm," Patricia said. "Decisions, decisions." Although the cheeseboard wasn't complete, she surveyed the other ingredients: baby pickles, green olives, and spicy mustard to accompany the German wine; candied pecan halves, honey roasted almonds, and dried apricots and cherries for the port. Slices of a sourdough baguette with some crispy bread sticks rounded out the assortment.

Patricia's brunette hair was tinted red and her lipstick matched the pink of her dress.

Over it she wore a black jacket that barely managed to cover her rotund form.

"I'll start with Riesling," she said, and held up a hand. "But I don't mind pouring for myself." She grinned, her plump cheeks rising. "You have very important business there."

Maris chuckled. "Then I'll just finish this up."

While being a food critic and sampling the offerings of all the finest restaurants might seem like a dream job, it carried an obvious downside as well—one with which Maris could sympathize. Though Patricia and she were the same height, the other woman was ten years her junior and easily fifty pounds heavier. The constant travel and eating pretty much guaranteed an unhealthy lifestyle.

"Ooh, the Riesling," Patricia murmured. "Very nice." She peered at the label. "Crown Winery."

"Just thirty minutes south of here," Maris said, adding the pecans to the board as a final touch. "The owner, Friedrich Krone, learned winemaking in Germany."

"Well, it shows," Patricia said.

Behind her the other two guests arrived. "Good evening, Andrew," Maris said, nodding to him and then his wife. "Melanie."

Wine in hand, Patricia had been headed to the sideboard to pick up a plate, but politely paused.

"Andrew and Melanie Yang," Maris said, "may I introduce Patricia Linn-Baker. Patricia, these are the Yangs."

The young Asian couple stepped forward, and Andrew shook Patricia's hand. "Pleased to meet you."

His wife did likewise. "Good to meet you."

"My pleasure," the food critic replied, "I'm sure."

If Maris had to guess, she'd put the young couple in their late twenties. Both wore glasses and were slim, and Melanie wore her straight black hair sweeping gracefully down to her shoulders.

Andrew took a moment to look at both bottles. "Hon, can I pour you the white wine?"

"Thanks, sweetie," she said, smiling. "I'll get us a plate."

As the two women made their selections, Maris poured some port for herself.

"You have a wonderful place here," Andrew said to her, as he finished pouring two Rieslings.

"Thank you," Maris said smiling. "I'm lucky enough to call it home."

His wife brought over a plate which she set down on the table, as she took her wine from him. "I imagine a property like this is a lot of work."

Maris grinned a little. "I'm just now beginning to figure that out."

As the guests enjoyed their food, Maris fetched a plate and gave herself an ample helping of the dried fruits and sweet nuts.

"Your eyeglasses," Patricia was saying to Melanie. "They're very stylish."

Maris had noticed them as well. Large and almost circular, the elegant frames were a pretty plum color.

"Thank you," Andrew replied, making both Maris and Patricia look at him. His wife gave him a playful thump on the arm, before she turned back to the food critic. "My husband, the optometrist."

"Ah," Patricia said, knowingly. When Maris joined them, the food critic pointed to the ricotta cheese on her plate. "This is wonderful, by the way. I have never come across ricotta on a cheeseboard before. Nicely done."

"High praise, indeed," Maris said, arching her brows. She gestured to the big woman, and said to the young couple, "Patricia is a food critic. You might have seen her columns in newspapers and magazines."

"Oh goodness," Melanie said, then turned to her husband. "I told you I thought she looked familiar."

As the quartet noshed and sipped, Patricia talked about her work and her current tour of the coast's eateries. The Yangs, it turned out, were celebrating their first anniversary. Andrew had surprised his wife with a paper airline ticket. Melanie was a high school science teacher, and they were making a quick trip before the new school year started.

Outside, the last rays of the setting sun were fading. Overnight the usual coastal fog would enshroud them. But for now, Maris simply enjoyed the warm atmosphere inside, and getting to know her guests.

7

The following morning, after the buffet and chores had been completed, Maris went back up to the optics house. Bear was already working on the outside walkway, cleaning the storm panes with a squeegee. Tall enough to reach their tops without a ladder, he worked carefully and methodically.

"Good morning," she mouthed and gave him a little wave, and he used the squeegee to wave back.

Inside, she saw that he had left the step ladder, microfiber cloths, and a pair of cotton gloves for her. She'd been careful not to wear any type of metal or jewelry, opting for terry cloth sweatpants and a simple t-shirt. It wasn't the most stylish of outfits but the safety of the optics outweighed everything else. For a moment, she considered her options. With all the pieces of glass, she wanted to make sure she didn't miss any. She would be methodical, like Bear. She would work in rows, starting at the top, circling around to complete the top tier, before proceeding to the next.

She moved the ladder into place, put the microfiber cloths on its top shelf, and picked up the gloves. But before she even got them on, she could see that they would be too big. They'd fit Bear, but she could fit both of her hands into a single glove. Though she was anxious to actually begin the job of cleaning the lens, she didn't want to risk not doing it right. At the back of the optics house, she opened the small door that was metal on the bottom and glass on the top, and stepped out onto the outer landing. She closed the door behind her—something that Aunt Glenda had drilled into her. Keeping the dust to a minimum was vital.

As she circled around to the front of the optics house, she tried to remember the last time she'd been out here. The fog had lifted although a slight haze hung in the air. The light breeze was cool and fresh and a gull cried out as it passed by. Bear was just finishing one panel as she approached. He set down the squeegee and picked up a rag.

"Bear?" Maris said. "You wouldn't happen to have another pair of gloves would you? A smaller pair."

His eyebrows arched over his soft brown eyes as he looked down at her hands. "Too big." Then he shook his head. "Those are the only ones." His gaze shifted to the fresnel lens, then quickly back to her. "Glenda had a pair, but I don't know where they are."

Maris thought for a moment. "Hmm." She'd never run across a pair of cotton gloves, or any nitrile ones for that matter. "I have no idea where they'd be." She gazed past the lens toward the house and beyond. "I think I'm just going to have to go into town and get some. I imagine the hardware store will have something."

At that, Bear dropped his rag next to his bucket. "I can go get them."

She waved him off. "Oh no, please. The last thing I want to do is slow you down due to my 'helping.' Besides, I might need to try them on."

Though he didn't say anything, she could guess what he was thinking: she might have a run-in with Rudy Schmid. She wasn't the type to court trouble, but she hadn't cared for his attitude at the picnic. Since she'd never actually spoken to him, it was hard to say what he was really like. Though she wasn't looking forward to it, maybe it was time to find out.

"I'll make sure to be quick," she said, and a thought occurred to her. "As long as I'm out, I can stop somewhere to pick up lunch. Any ideas?"

"Pizza del Popolo?" he said quickly.

She grinned at him. "Sounds great. I'll be right back."

8

By the time Maris arrived at the pizzeria, the sun was out in all its glory. It lit the narrow interior of the restaurant, bathing it in warm hues. The polished wood counter gleamed as did the two metal stools off to the side, parked at a narrow shelf that served as a tiny dining area. It wasn't difficult to see to the back of the space, lined with brick ovens, gleaming metal work surfaces, and a large grill. But the owner was nowhere in sight.

"Hello?" Maris called out. "Anybody here?"

"Hello!" came the immediate reply from somewhere on the other side of the counter, maybe the floor.

Maris took a step closer and peered over

it. Max was on his knees, in front of the first oven. Maris hadn't realized before that the area underneath each one was stacked with small logs of wood.

He dusted off his hands and sprang up. "Ah, *Bella*," he said smiling at her, making his crooked nose crinkle. "*Buongiorno.*"

"Good morning," she said, eying the charcoal smudge on his chef's shirt. Then she regarded the oven. "Trouble in pizza paradise?"

His smile faltered. "The oven," he said. "It broke this morning."

"Oh no," she said, "broke?"

He pointed at the circular temperature indicator on its front, then tugged on his cauliflower ear. "It cannot maintain temperature."

Maris frowned at it. "Pretty important for an oven."

"Yes," he said turning to it. He waved an arm toward the rest of the narrow space. "Even in my tiny restaurant, I have another, *naturalmente*. But a pizzeria with only one oven?" He tsked. "Like playing *bocce* without enough balls." He looked back at her as though she'd just walked in. "But you did not come here to hear of my woes." He beamed at her and his smile was infectious. "What can I do for you?"

"I'd like to order lunch," she said. Although she pulled one of the paper menus from the display, she already knew the short list of items and what she would order. She laid it on the counter and pointed to her selections. "Four Calzone Vesuvios and the Creamy Caesar Salad."

"*Eccelente*," he said. "Coming right up."

"No hurry," she added quickly. "I've got to go next door and find some gloves."

He seemed as though he was going to turn away and get the meals started, but then paused. For a moment, he looked at her, and then looked away.

"Yes, Max?" she said.

He wrung his hands together. "Have you heard about the autopsy report for Joy?"

She gave him a sympathetic smile and shook her head. "No. I'm afraid not. But I'll let you know when I do."

His smile returned, and he bowed a little. "Thank you. Lunch will be ready when you return."

9

———

Superior Hardware lived up to its name. The moment Maris stepped in, it was like entering another world. The store's aisles came right up to the entrance, with a small counter off to the side that had a cash register. Each aisle was labelled with a small sign at the top with names like "Electrical," "Plumbing," and "Hardware."

"Hardware," she muttered, frowning a little.

Wasn't the entire store a hardware store?

No one was at the cash register, nor did she hear anyone in conversation—and had to admit she was a little relieved. It'd be good to have a little look around before getting tossed

out by the owner. She picked the aisle labelled "Hardware."

As soon as she entered it, she understood.
Hardware meant cabinet and door hardware.
Each area was clearly marked and there were
even little drawings attached to the pull-out
bins, showing you what was inside. It was
clean, and neat, and not what she'd expected
at all. For a few moments she simply took it
all in, slowly ambling up the aisle. At its end
she saw that the store was divided into two
sections, and another set of aisles waited at
the back. In the corner, she glimpsed a staircase that presumably led up to a second
story.

"Can I help you find something?" said a
male voice, startling her from behind.

She jumped a little and turned, hand to
chest. "Uh, yes."

But the man who stood in front of her
wasn't Rudy Schmid. This man was considerably younger and considerably more muscu-
lar. If it wasn't for the baggy hardware store
shirt, she'd have said that he was a profes-
sional weight lifter.

"I need to get some gloves," she said,
noticing the soul patch on his chin, the small

scar near his eye, and the tattoos on his neck. "Either soft cotton or nitrile."

"Then we want to look in 'Workwear'," he said smiling. "This way."

As he headed toward the back of the store, he angled off for the stairs. Like his shirt, his work pants were a bit big for him, and Maris could see that the back of his neck was tattooed as well. He wore his red hair cropped so short, he looked almost bald.

"What do you need the gloves for?" he asked, when he reached the second story.

It was equally packed with many aisles of goods.

"I'm going to be cleaning some glass," she said, following him into one of the aisles and passing a few other shoppers. "The fresnel lens at the lighthouse."

"Oh really?" he said, sounding interested. "That's a new one."

Maris laughed a little. "You can say that again."

"Here we are," he said and pointed to a stack of boxes of nitrile gloves. "I'm afraid we don't have cotton gloves in stock, but if the nitrile will do, we've got those." He regarded her. "So, are you in charge of the lighthouse?"

Maris smiled and extended her hand. "Maris Seaver," she said. "I'm the owner of the lighthouse and the attached B&B."

"Oh wow," he said. "Pleased to meet you." He daintily took her hand by just the fingers. "Guy Koch."

The calluses on his big hands felt like sandpaper and Maris was glad for the lady's handshake. "Good to meet you, Guy."

She looked at the boxes. "Well, I know that extra large and large aren't going to fit."

He picked up the one marked medium and handed it to her. "These will be perfect."

"Great," she said, looking at it more closely. "They're purple?"

He grimaced a little. "I'm afraid so. That's the only color we have in medium. In fact, it's the last box."

"Oh not a problem at all," she said smiling. "I think purple is going to be pretty."

"Oh, okay," he said, smiling as well. "Is there anything else I can help you with?"

Maris shook her head. "I think that's it."

"Then I'll ring you up," he said, turning back toward the stairs.

As she followed him down, she got a better view of the first floor. Though she hadn't seen them before, there were a few shoppers scattered in the many aisles. But the person she didn't see was the owner.

"Is Mr. Schmid here today?" she asked as they headed to the register.

Guy glanced over his shoulder. "He's here every day. But right now he's on the dock in the back doing inventory, and has been all morning. Did you want to speak to him?"

Maris shook her head as she put her box of gloves on the counter next to the stack of green, white, and red coupons for Pizza del Popolo's grand opening. "It's nothing urgent. I just thought I'd introduce myself, since I've never been in the store before." Guy aimed the scanner at the price tag. "I understand he's a bit...gruff with his female clients." She handed over her credit card.

"Well," Guy said quietly. "I don't know if I'd say that." He slid the card through the reader. "It's more like he treats them like he would a man."

"Hmm," Maris said. That wasn't how it appeared at the picnic. But Maris decided not to press the point. Guy was his employee, after all. She signed the credit card slip.

"Would you like a bag?" he asked, reaching under the counter.

"No," she said, stowing her card in the wallet and dropping it into her purse. "The box is fine."

He handed it to her with a smile. "Nice to meet you, and thanks for shopping at Superior Hardware."

She took the gloves, and smiled back. "Thanks for your help, Guy, and nice to meet you too."

10

───────

Maris carried the cardboard box of amazing smelling Italian food through the living room and out onto the side porch. She set it down on the table and headed to where Cookie was working in the garden. Today it looked like she was pruning and collecting some herbs. A small basket on the ground beside her was full of fresh cuttings.

"Lunch is on," Maris called to her from the garden's edge. "I'll go get Bear."

Cookie waved back. "I'll put some tea on. I think Bear is still up in the lighthouse."

Maris glanced up to see him looking down at them. She waved him down and pointed to the porch. He wasted no time in disappearing from view.

As Maris unpacked the box, she saw that Max had provided all the napkins and plastic cutlery as well. Each calzone was in its own wax coated, paper box and, if Maris was careful, she could spoon some of the creamy Caesar salad into each. She was just finishing when Cookie returned with a tray of three tea cups.

She nodded at the boxes of golden brown calzones. "Those look amazing."

"They smell even better," Maris agreed. "The drive home seemed longer than usual."

By the time Cookie had distributed the tea, Bear had joined them. "Calzone Vesuvio," she said, and pushed one of the boxes toward him. She handed him a fork, knife, and napkin. "With a creamy Caesar salad on the side."

Like a small pizza that had been folded in half, the semi-circular dough had been crimped on the round edge and slit on top. Tomato sauce and cheese had bubbled from the slim openings.

As the three took their seats, Bear said, "Thank you."

"Yes," Cookie said. "Thanks for picking these up." She took one of the large croutons from the salad, and popped it in her mouth. "Mmm," she said chewing. "Just the right amount of garlic in that dressing and…" She speared the tender romaine with her fork. "…a hint of anchovy paste. Classic." She took a bite of the salad. "Mmm hmm."

Her interest piqued, Maris tried the salad too, while Bear carved into the calzone. Max had used a light touch on the tangy dressing, and added curled shavings of Parmesan that were as big as the oversized croutons. If she'd simply ordered a whole salad for herself, that probably would have been enough.

"Mmm," Bear said, covering his mouth with one of the little napkins. "Just like my grandmother used to make." He nodded as he chewed. "Egg in the middle."

"Egg?" Maris said, astonished. She peered at his calzone. In the center was a whole egg that looked as though it'd been poached in the middle of the sauce and cheeses.

"Is that traditional?" Cookie asked, as she cut into hers.

Bear shook his head and picked up his tea. "It depends on the region."

Maris decided not to start at the end, but cut right into the center. She was immediately rewarded with the sight of the yellow yolk. "This is amazing," she muttered. She took a forkful and gave it a try.

Though the ingredients were much the same as in pizza, Maris knew from the menu that the delicious baked calzone had three kinds of cheese: mozzarella, ricotta, and pecorino. Combined with the zesty tomato sauce and egg, the texture of it was incredibly smooth.

"Anchovies," Cookie said, sounding surprised and then she grinned. "No salt needed."

Maris took a sip of her tea. "Perfect compliment to the salad too."

The chef nodded in agreement. "He certainly knows his stuff."

Bear had finished with his first calzone, but didn't take the next. Instead, he sat back in his chair and patted his stomach. "Very tasty."

Maris eyed him. "There's another for you, Bear."

But the big man shook his head. "I was so hungry." He patted his tummy again. "But now I'm full."

Maris's eyebrows flew up, even as she had

another bite of salad. She'd never seen Bear stop at a single helping—of anything.

"I was hungry too," Cookie said, "and tired. But now I think I'll finish pruning the rest of the garden." She paused for a moment, and stared down at the food. Then she looked at Maris. "And you, Maris? How are you feeling now that you've eaten?"

Maris looked down at the half-finished calzone and salad, and thought for a moment. "Relaxed," she said. She glanced in the direction of town. "I didn't realize it at the time, but I think the visit to Superior Hardware had me stressed out."

Cookie nodded. "I can understand that." She gazed at all their meals and smirked. "But isn't it interesting that all three of us got exactly what we needed?"

"It is," Maris agreed, gazing down at her lunch. She really did feel calm. "I wonder..."

"If Max is one of the magick folk?" Bear finished for her. He looked at Cookie, who nodded.

"It's like my tea," the chef said, with a tinge of awe in her voice. "I've never run across the same talent in a cook."

"So no matter what ails you," Maris said,

"even if it's just being hungry, Max's food is exactly what you need."

Bear shrugged. "But it also tastes good."

Cookie laughed. "Oh that's for sure. The pizzeria is going to be a wonderful addition to the town."

"If he can keep his ovens running," Maris said.

Bear sat forward. "Are they broken?"

Maris nodded. "One of them. Something about a draft and uneven heating. He wasn't having any luck with it."

"Hmm," Bear said. He glanced up at the lighthouse, then back to Cookie and Maris. "I finished cleaning the storm panes, so maybe I'll see if I can't help Max?"

Maris smiled at him. "I'm sure he'd appreciate any help you could give him. Thank you, Bear."

Cookie started to fold the top of her box over the remains of her food. "Maybe you should take your other calzone with you," she said to Bear. "In case it gets late by the time you're done." She finished her tea. "And I think I'll go tackle the rest of that garden."

"And I'll get back to the lens," Maris said, "now that I've got the gloves."

All three got to their feet, picking up their boxes.

"Sounds like a plan," Cookie said. She paused for a moment as she picked up her leftovers. "Excellent lunch."

11

Maris took her time with the microfiber cloth. On the step ladder to reach the highest elements of the fresnel lens, she carefully smoothed the soft, dry material from one edge of the element to the other. As she passed over it, just the barest hint of a brighter gleam greeted her. There wasn't much dust on it but there was some. She folded the edge of the cloth so as not to contaminate the rest of the glass with its dust, and gently swiped in the opposite direction.

"Think of it like painting," Bear had told her. "Nice and easy."

For several minutes she simply wiped off one piece after another. But as she thought back to purchasing the purple nitrile gloves she was wearing, she suddenly remembered Max. He'd been worried about the cause of Joy's death.

She set down the cloth, descended the ladder, and backed away from the optics. Only then did she take out her phone. Mac picked up right away.

"Good afternoon," he said, and she heard the smile in his voice.

"Good afternoon," she said grinning. They'd been on a half-a-dozen dates at this point, and were settling into a pleasant familiarity.

"How are things over at the B&B today?" he asked.

"Actually, I'm in the lighthouse. Bear showed me how to clean the fresnel lens. I'm trying to learn more about the technical aspects of being a lightkeeper."

"Good for you," he said. "It sounds like a bit of work."

Maris looked at the stack of clean cloths waiting for her. She had at least a few hours of cleaning ahead. "It is that, but it's also fun to learn something new."

"I agree," Mac said. "It helps keep things fresh."

"Exactly," she said, and paused, trying to segue smoothly to the autopsy results.

"You want to know about the coroner's report," the sheriff said.

Maris laughed. "Am I so obvious?"

She heard papers rustle. "Obvious is not a word I'd ever apply to you." There was silence for a moment. "Here we go. They found botulinum toxin in her system, and also in the homemade salsa that she had at the picnic. No other poisons or underlying medical conditions were discovered. She was in good health."

"Other than ingesting a neurotoxin," Maris said.

"Other than that," Mac agreed.

"And was all the other food tested?"

"Yes," he said. "The bento lunches, the pizza, Joy's other food. Everything else was clear. It's a miracle that there wasn't cross-contamination."

Maris exhaled a little with relief. Max would be glad to know. "That's for sure. From what Lucille said, it would have taken so little to be lethal."

"Exactly," he said. "We're about to head to Ms. Castro's house right now as a matter of fact. See if we can determine how the salsa became contaminated."

"Then I won't hold you up," she said.

"You're not holding me up," he said. "Well, maybe just a little. It's always a pleasure when you call."

Maris found herself grinning again. "I'm glad to hear it."

There was an awkward pause. "I'll get going then."

But a thought occurred to her. "Are you going to Max's grand opening?"

"I hadn't really thought about it," he said.

"I'll be there," she told him.

"Then I'll most definitely be going," he said, and she heard that smile in his voice again.

"Great," she said. "Then it's a date."

WORKING STEADILY, though in no hurry, Maris found a good rhythm for the repetitive task. As she smiled to herself, she wondered if she'd stumbled upon the Zen of lighthouse maintenance. It was quiet work and calming. Surrounded by breathtaking views in every direction, she instead focused her attention on the center of her little glass world. Piece by piece, she whittled away at the task, folding the cloth, cleaning a section, and moving the ladder.

Now she stood on the platform, working on the pieces toward the middle. Although her back ached a bit, and her arms were getting tired, she didn't mind. There was no hurry to get it all done in one day.

But as she swiped the cloth over one of the pieces, it began to sparkle. Tiny points of multi-colored light seemed to dance inside it.

"Wow," she muttered, realizing what was happening. Claribel was giving her a remote viewing. Maris had often appealed to the magical being of the lighthouse, hoping for some insight into a crime. But she wasn't investigating anything right now.

Nevertheless, her vision was taken over by a closeup view of a tiny office. It was little more than a closet and it was a mess. Papers of all types littered an old metal desk. An out-of-date computer monitor was on it as well. Some cardboard boxes were scattered on the floor.

Not only did she not recognize this place, she didn't know why it was being shown.

Then the remote viewing winked out in a tiny puff of sparkles.

Her brows knit together as she gazed up at the fresnel lens. Why in the world was Claribel showing her some dingy, little office?

"Is there trouble there, Old Girl?" she asked.

But of course there was no answer. And really Maris knew the answer anyway. There was trouble there. Otherwise Claribel wouldn't have shown her.

She regarded the entire assembly of steel and glass. "Thanks," she said. "I don't know what it means but thanks."

But as Maris returned to the cleaning, her mind wandered back to the only dead body she'd seen—Joy Castro. But Mac had told her only this afternoon that she'd died of food poisoning. She thought back to the picnic, the argument, Jill Maxwell doing CPR, the ambulance, the Pages, and finally Mac and Rudy.

At a good stopping point, she stood back and surveyed her work. The heart of the Old Girl was starting to look magnificent and

Maris had to smile. If this wasn't rewarding, she didn't know the meaning of the word. As she gathered her dirty cloths, she also came to a decision. It was time to look in on Minako and Alfred. She could see how they were doing after the death of their friend—and maybe ask a few questions about her.

12

———

Though Maris had gone to her bedroom to change out of the work clothes, she took a little detour to the seat of the bay window. Her pudgy little cat was curled up in the sun but raised his head when she approached. He gave her a tiny, tinny, harmonica-like meow.

"Hey there, Mojo," she said quietly, stroking the silky fur on top of his head. "Catching some rays?" His big amber eyes looked up at her, all the brighter against his jet black coat. He pushed his head against her palm, and she obliged with some scratches behind his velvety ears. "Don't bake over here, okay?" His only answer was a purr. She smiled as he closed his eyes. "You're welcome."

She went to the armoire, selected a new set of clothes, and changed into them. Like her aunt, she favored skirts and blouses. The aqua top with its ruffled collar complimented her blue eyes, as well as matching the small floral print on the cream-colored skirt. But as she stepped into the usual low heels that were her go-to for visiting the Towne Plaza, she felt something moving inside one.

With a small shriek, she jumped back. Although she landed awkwardly, with one foot in a shoe and one foot bare, she managed to stay upright. Mojo flew past her toward the shoes.

"No, Mojo!" she gasped and made a grab for him—only catching air.

What if it was some sort of reptile or rodent? She didn't want it to hurt him, and vice versa.

But by the time she picked him up, he had it in his mouth. "Drop it," she ordered, just as she saw what it was. "Oh no," she muttered and reached for it. "Really, Mojo?"

Quickly, she grasped the tarot card, but he didn't let go. "Mojo," she said, her voice stern. His big amber eyes looked up at her, though he didn't open his mouth. "If you don't let that go, there'll be no snack for you tonight." He blinked at her and his jaw dropped open. She smiled at him and nodded. "That's my good boy."

As she set him down, he gave a brief little mew.

"Yes, yes," she told him. "I'm looking at it now."

It was the seven of swords. A man carrying five swords in his arms was looking over at the two upright swords he'd apparently left behind. He appeared to be near a military encampment and he was definitely skulking away. His satisfied grin said he'd got away with something.

Maris tapped her temple and used her photographic memory to look at the tarot interpretation booklet. The seven of swords was the card most associated with criminal activity. The man with the swords was up to no good.

"Hmm," Maris said. "Another clue." She looked down to where the little cat sat cleaning his face. "But to what?" Now he ignored her.

She returned her attention to the card and frowned. First Claribel, and now Mojo.

Something was definitely going on. It was time to get to town and do some snooping.

As he watched, she reached down and gave him a little tap on the head with the card. "Thanks, Mojo."

13

At Inklings New & Used Books, Maris found Alfred helping a customer, while Minako was at the register ringing up someone's purchase. At least the death at the picnic hadn't put people off shopping. As she waited for them to be free, she went to the dispenser with the complimentary apple cider, and poured some into one of the paper cups. As she sipped it and sauntered slowly toward the books, she admired the gorgeous display of indoor plants that covered the brick wall behind the counter and ran the entire length of the store. How they managed to get them to thrive in their little baskets, suspended from hooks, Maris had no idea. But she suspected that a good deal of time was spent watering.

Still waiting, Maris went to the main display table where the new books were usually found.

When she'd trotted the globe for her hospitality career, she'd always had a good book with her. Whenever possible, she'd try to find something that took place in whatever part of the world she happened to be in. Often they were novels, but occasionally non-fiction was nice too. Today it seemed the theme of the display was coffee table books. With their big glossy covers that had amazing images, Maris was immediately captivated.

"*The Secret Life of Redwoods,*" she read out loud, touching it. The cover showed a thick forest of the giant trees, not unlike those just east of town. Their crowns seemed to converge in the center of the photo, with just a glimpse of a bright blue sky above them. Shafts of sunlight sliced at diagonals across their red, rough, and massive trunks. Inside the book, the very first picture was of a tiny seedling, bathing in light. It would have looked at home in Cookie's garden. A slender brown stem was topped with four thin leaves, fanning out like a palm tree. It was hard to believe that it could grow to such an enormous size.

"Maris," Alfred said. "I thought that was you. Can I help you find something?"

She smiled at him. "Not at all," she said, picking up the book and tucking it under her arm. "I think I've found it."

He glanced at the cover as she finished her cider. "That's an excellent choice. The author tells the most amazing story of their life cycles, as though they were people, not plants. I've certainly never looked at them the same way since reading it."

"I'm looking forward to sitting down with it," she said. "But actually, I wasn't really here to shop. I just wanted to stop by and see how you and Minako were holding up. You know, after yesterday."

He grimaced a little. "Well, I think Nurse Maxwell is probably going to block my number soon. But she's really been wonderful, answering all of our questions. I start to cough, probably because I'm dusting, and I wonder if that's a symptom of something, so I call her."

Maris gave him an understanding smile.

"I'm sure I'd do the same, and I'm equally sure Jill is fine with it."

Minako joined them then. "Fine with what?" she said, looking inquisitively between them.

"With my calling her every five minutes," Alfred said.

Minako put a hand on his arm. "I know. Both of us." She looked at Maris. "I had a stomachache, probably from all the worry, and Alfred was kind enough to call." She took a phone from her back pocket. "And I've been searching the internet..."

"...for all kinds of food poisoning," Alfred said.

"It was botulism," Maris told them. "They found the toxin in the salsa."

Minako gasped a little as her eyes went wide, but covered her mouth.

"So the forensics person was right," Alfred said.

"Lucille Trahan," Maris said, "the senior investigator. Yes, she called it."

Minako shook her head, as her eyes misted up. "Poor Joy. She was much too young."

Alfred nodded as his arm went around

his wife's shoulders. "And so full of life. We're..." He used a finger behind his glasses to wipe a tear from his eye.

"We're going to miss her," Minako said.

Maris sighed. "I'm so sorry for your loss," she said. Though she'd come here to ask questions about their friend, this was clearly not the time. The shock of her death—and witnessing it—had obviously hit them hard.

"You know the worst thing?" Minako said quietly.

Maris shook her head. "No."

Minako looked up at Alfred, who whispered, "We feel like we've dodged a bullet."

"We feel so lucky to be alive," she said, then covered her eyes with both hands. "It's awful."

Maris put a hand on her arm. "Listen to me." She glanced at Alfred. "Both of you. It's never wrong to feel good about being alive. You feel lucky, because you are lucky. Not just at avoiding a neurotoxin, but also that you have each other."

Minako wiped her eyes, and managed a smile. "True."

Alfred nodded quickly. "All true." He

smiled down at his wife. "She'd have been glad for us, you know?"

She looked up and genuinely smiled at him. "I do know." She stood up a little straighter and Alfred let her go. Together, they took in a deep breath of air and looked at Maris. "Thank you," they both said.

"I didn't do a thing," she said. Then she hefted the book and grinned. "Except find my next read."

"If you're ready," Minako said. "I'd be happy to ring you up."

"Sounds good," Maris said, and followed her to the counter.

14

Before going back to her car, Maris decided to check Pizza del Popolo. Since Bear's truck was nowhere in sight, she assumed he was finished. Inside the bright pizzeria, Max was humming something that sounded operatic while he chopped fresh tomatoes. He was just placing them in an enormous metal pot on the stove when she stepped up to the counter.

"*Ciao, Bella!*" he said, grinning. "Twice in one day?" He waggled a finger at her. "I'm going to make you Italian."

Maris smiled and set down her book. "Actually, I'm not here for your glorious food. I was wondering if Bear managed to help you out?"

The Italian chef cocked his head back.

"Help me? Help me? Help is the understatement." He grasped the black metal door of the oven by both its handles, removed it, and stood aside. "Look." He pointed to a spot at the bottom of the oven's dome. "Good as new."

Maris could see a slightly different color of mortar and what looked like two new bricks, much thinner than the rest. The late afternoon sun that slanted through the front windows illuminated it like a spotlight.

"Oh, look at that," she exclaimed. "So the problem was the bricks?"

Max shook his head. "The mortar, but he had to take the bricks out. He explained everything perfectly. The bricks had to be destroyed to get to the mortar."

"Ah," Maris said. "He does do a great job of explaining."

"A natural born teacher," Max agreed, "and a problem-solver."

"Problem-solver?" she said, cocking her head and looking again at the repair.

Max measured his hand against one of the old bricks. "Superior Hardware didn't have the original style brick, or the mortar either. So Bear made his own mixture, and used the small bricks that they had to make it work."

Though the new, thinner bricks no longer matched the rest of the oven, if it worked, it worked. Bear had obviously been meticulous in placing the new material to match the contour of the dome and the new mortar had been used sparingly and neatly.

"That's fabulous," Maris said, wondering how many times the consummate handyman had been a problem-solver at the B&B.

Max pointed to the narrow space at the back of the oven. "The big Bear had to find a way to get himself in there to really take a good look."

Maris regarded the small area. It would have been tight. "Wow." She couldn't quite imagine it.

"I told him that if he needed to knock down that wall, he had my permission." Max gave her a wry smile. "Maybe my restaurant could be wider."

Maris chuckled as she gazed at it. "No doubt the hardware store would be happy to donate the space to you."

For a few moments they both simply gazed at the repair work, Max smiling broadly as he crossed his arms over his chest. In the back of the domed oven, a small pile of wood logs and kindling was waiting. Just above that area, a metal pipe emerged and went straight up to the ceiling.

"I invited him to stay for dinner," the chef said, "but he said he likes to be home before dark."

"Right," Maris said. Cookie had let her know that their handyman was a shifter. Though Maris didn't know the details, it was somehow good for him not to be out at night. "He likes to start early and finish early."

Max nodded and returned his gaze to the repair. "I am to let it set for twenty four hours, then heat it, but not too high. The next day, it can get a little hotter. It has to cure."

"Just in time," Maris said. She paused for a moment. "I also wanted to let you know that the autopsy report has come back."

At that, the Italian chef's smile vanished, making his crooked nose seem even more bent. His dark eyes peered at her. "And?"

"Joy Castro died of botulinum toxin that was present in her homemade salsa," Maris said. "None of the other food was tainted in the least, including your pizza."

He closed his eyes and exhaled. "*Uff*," he muttered and fingered his cauliflower ear.

Maris smiled at the nervous gesture and gave him a moment to savor the good news. "There was never any doubt."

He looked at her, his big smile returning. "Thank you, *Bella*."

She gave the new repair a final look. "I've got to get back to the B&B for the evening wine and cheese."

"And I must return to my tomato sauce," he said.

As she turned to go, she said, "I'll catch you later."

"*Ciao, Bella*," he called out.

15

In the morning, Maris was up earlier than usual. Even so, as she got dressed, she could smell the aromas of breakfast wafting from the kitchen. Cookie had likely been up for at least an hour, in her element. Mojo, however, was not yet ready for the day. He still lay curled up on the bed in the spot that she'd vacated.

As she gave him a gentle pet, she turned off the nightstand's Tiffany lamp. "See you in a bit," she said quietly. Eyes closed, he simply sighed in return.

In the kitchen, Cookie was just moving the last quiche dish into the bottom oven. When she stood, she adjusted her apron and smiled at Maris. "Good morning."

"Good morning," Maris said, peeking

through the oven glass. "Is that what I think it is?"

Cookie eyed her. "Let me guess. Your favorite?"

Maris gave her a mock scowl. "I don't even know what's in it."

The diminutive chef grinned as she went to the stove. "It's my Japanese Quiche."

"Oh," Maris exclaimed. She knew it by heart. "Eggs, shiitake and enoki mushrooms, spinach, sharp Cheddar and Monterey Jack cheeses, and just a hint of that lovely bunching onion." Maris peered into the oven again. "My favorite," she whispered.

Cookie chuckled. "There's some tea brewing in that kettle. And you can grate some potatoes for the hash browns whenever you're ready."

"Tea first," Maris said. "Can I make a cup for you?"

"That'd be great," the chef said, as she got her mixer ready. "Did Max get his oven back up and running?"

Maris retrieved two tea cups from the cupboard. "He's already firing it up. There's a process called curing where he needs to fire it higher and higher each day. Bear got it patched up quite nicely, and Max should have the oven ready for the grand opening."

"Good to hear," Cookie said, as she began to add ingredients to the mixer bowl.

As Maris put just a bit of lemon into the tea, Cookie poured flour into the bowl. Baking powder, sugar, and salt followed.

"Here you go," Maris said, bringing over the cup and setting it on the counter.

"Thanks," Cookie said, and added the milk and vegetable oil.

She paused for a moment as they both took a sip. Maris had instantly recognized the earthy and woody aroma of the ginseng tea. The addition of the honey—a gift from Bear —added just the right amount of sweetness.

"That's going to go well with the quiche," Maris said.

The diminutive chef grinned at her. "Exactly what I was thinking."

When she returned to the mixer, she added the spices. It looked like this morning they were also serving Belgian waffles.

Maris peeled the potatoes, grated them, and used dish towels to remove the excess moisture from them. Then she fetched the fresh berries, and added them to a large china bowl with a serving spoon. Cookie had just finished the batter and set it aside.

"I think we'll put out the DIY-Waffle-Flip-and-Cook iron today. Let the guests have a little fun with making fresh waffles."

Maris brought over the uncooked hash browns. "That sounds great. I'll go set it up."

As the distant sun slowly lit the gray mist surrounding the B&B, Maris brought each of the finished buffet foods to the warming trays on the dining room's sideboard: slices of the Japanese quiche, with its super flavorful mushrooms; crispy hash browns; the fresh berries, as well as toast and the Belgian waffle batter. Maple and raspberry syrup stood by, as did a bowl of whipped cream from the dairy in Cheeseman Village.

Not surprisingly, Patricia was the first one down. The food critic surveyed the sideboard with a smile. Then she glanced at Cookie. "I followed my nose. It never fails. Few people really appreciate how one of the most important elements in good food is the aroma. It can tell you so much about what you're about to experience." She picked up a plate. "And my nose tells me that we are in for something wonderful."

Maris winked at Cookie, who waggled her eyebrows a bit. Both of them waited as the big woman went immediately to the waffle maker. As she poured in the batter, Maris motioned for Cookie to precede her. The chef served herself a slice of the quiche and some berries. Maris did likewise.

As Patricia waited for the waffle iron, she peered closely at the quiche. "Wait a minute," she said and looked behind her at Cookie. "Are those Japanese mushrooms?"

Cookie nodded. "And bunching onions too."

Just then the waffle maker dinged and Patricia flipped the iron over.

"Good morning," said Andrew from the doorway.

"More early risers," Maris said to Andrew and Melanie. "Good morning." She motioned to the sideboard. "Please help yourself. There's fresh coffee in the carafe and hot water in the dispenser. Cookie has some of her ginseng blend in those infusers."

"I'd adore some morning ginseng," Melanie said. She paused and looked at her husband. "Coffee for you, sweetie?"

"Yep," he said. "I've got to have that morning jolt."

As they moved to the sideboard, Patricia removed her golden browned waffle from the iron with a fork, then put a dollop of whipped cream on the side, and filled the little openings with maple syrup. If Maris was having one, she'd do exactly the same. Then the critic fetched herself a glass of orange juice and joined Cookie at the dining room table.

"Do I smell nutmeg?" she asked, her face clearly delighted.

"You do," Cookie answered. "That's quite an accurate sense of smell you've got. Most people would have guessed sugar."

But Patricia was too busy to make a reply. As she took her first bite of the waffle, Cookie speared a strawberry with her fork and Maris tried hard not to watch the food critic. The woman's brows furrowed and for a moment, Maris felt a knot of dread drop in her stomach. But as Patricia chewed and eagerly cut another piece, she nodded.

Finally she said, "The vanilla and cinnamon together with the nutmeg..." She dipped the second piece in the whipped cream. "It's...it's just beautiful."

Maris exhaled a little, and Cookie simply nodded.

Andrew had also made a waffle for himself, but Melanie returned with a slice of quiche. But as they'd done at the Wine Down, they shared both plates.

"What have you two got planned for today?" Maris asked.

"Well," Andrew said, "inspired by the wine and cheese last night, we're going to go take the tour at Alegra Winery."

"Mmm," Maris said, setting down her tea. "That's a wonderful tour. I'd have to say that their tasting room is one of the most generous, in terms of wine and food, that I've ever come across." She smiled at them. "Which is saying something, so I'm sure you'll enjoy it."

"Oh my god," Melanie said. "This quiche is amazing." Patricia's head whipped around so fast that her bangs fell in her eyes. "Honey," the young woman said to her husband, "have you tried this?" She used the side of her fork to cut off a piece and offered it to him, placing the morsel into his mouth.

"The cheese is fresh from the Cheeseman

Village Dairy," Maris told them.

"Wow," Andrew said nodding.

"Right," Patricia said, almost shooting up from her seat. "I've got to try that."

In another few moments she was at the sideboard serving herself a piece. She held it up in front of her, examining it from all sides. Then she put it directly under her nose and inhaled deeply.

"Ginger?" she asked.

"Very good," Cookie said.

Patricia took a bite. For several long moments she simply stood there chewing and examining the slice with her fork. "Delicious," she finally said. "Just a hint of soy sauce."

"From the shiitake," Cookie confirmed.

As the big woman brought her plate back to the table, she said, "I'm on a tour of the coast's eateries, but it seems that overlooking this B&B has been quite the oversight." She was looking at her plate and sounded as if she was thinking out loud. As Maris and Cookie exchanged a satisfied look, the food critic added, "I wonder what my editor would say about broadening the definition of a restaurant."

16

Once the dishwasher was loaded, Maris was headed to her room to check on Mojo when the hallway went completely white.

"Again?" she said quietly. It was a precognitive vision. "But why?" As she put a hand to the wall to steady herself, a blurry image came into focus. "Superior Hardware."

Why was she not surprised?

As though she was standing in the Towne Plaza, she watched as the coroner removed a gurney with a black body bag on it from the front of the store. Meanwhile, the forensics team passed him on their way inside. Some onlookers on the sidewalk, heads together, were pointing at the coroner's van.

Dread welled up in Maris's chest, and she

put a hand to it. Someone at Superior Hardware was going to die. But before she could tell who, the vision winked out. She was staring at her open bedroom door. In the next instant, she dashed through it, startled Mojo on the bed, and then grabbed her phone and purse.

"Sorry, Mojo," she gasped.

For a moment she considered calling the store, or maybe even Mac. But the first problem would be that no one would believe her. The second problem would arise when someone died, and it appeared that she knew.

As she ran back into the hallway, she almost collided with Cookie, who deftly moved aside.

"Whoa," the older woman said, her back to the wall and clutching a rag to her chest.

"Sorry!" Maris called back over her shoulder. "Someone's going to die at Superior Hardware."

17

Encouraged by the fact that no coroner's van was parked in front of the store, Maris hastily parked and ran inside—only to be brought up short. Guy was helping a customer in the aisle directly in front of her, and they both looked up at her in surprise.

"Maris," he said. "Are you okay?"

Her momentum carried her another half step before she could stop. "Yes," she said, a bit breathless. She took a moment to adjust the purse on her shoulder. "I'm fine," she said too quickly, "and you?"

He smiled a little. "We're good here, I think." He glanced at his customer, an older man, who nodded and shrugged.

"Good," Maris said, pushing her hair

back a bit. "Good." As they continued to stare at her, she added, "I'll just, um, have a look around."

"Okay," Guy said. "If you need any help, just let me know." He turned back to the older man. "They're normally in Aisle Fourteen."

As they ambled off, Maris watched them go, and took a good look at the store. Nothing seemed out of place and neither Guy nor his customer appeared alarmed in the least—unless it was at her. Taking her time, she went back to the stairs in the corner. She climbed them almost all the way to the top, then stopped and surveyed the first floor. Two more customers were browsing at its edge in the lighting section.

"Hmm," she muttered.

There was no way to know when the precognitive vision might actually become reality. Often in the course of an investigation, she'd see its relevance as facts unfolded. But she'd never seen a death before it happened.

Up on the second floor, it was also business as usual, though there were no customers. To her relief, there were also no bodies on the floor. She went to the stairs and started down, noticing the hallway in the other corner of the large space. She'd just take a peek in there, before going back home.

Careful to avoid Guy, she quietly approached the hallway. A directional sign for the bathroom was at its end. As she passed it, she thought again of letting Mac know. Though he wasn't one of the magick folk— and the unwritten rule of Pixie Point Bay dictated silence when it came to normals—this was a case of life and death. For all she knew, he wouldn't even believe her. But if there was even the slightest chance that her gift could save a life, shouldn't she reveal it?

Maris grimaced at the thought and found herself near the end of the short hallway. To her right was the door marked 'Restroom.' Ahead was an unlabelled door that presumably led to the alley behind and the store's loading dock. To her left was a door with a drab and crooked little sign that read 'Office.' She checked over her shoulder to make sure no one saw her, and then quickly opened the door, stepped in, and closed it behind her.

"Oh," she said. "Excuse me. I must have..." Her voice trailed off as she stared at Rudy Schmid's hunched back. His face was turned away from her and he apparently hadn't heard her come in.

Was he taking a nap?

Quietly she crept forward. He was slumped on top of a metal desk, which she recognized immediately. This was the office that Claribel had shown her. In front of him was the old computer as well. He'd apparently been working. She had to be on the right trail. But as the seriousness of that realization dawned, it also occurred to her where she was: a small and confined space. In addition to being worried about being caught snooping around, the anxiety of her mild claustrophobia piled on top of it.

If Rudy was napping, that was too bad.

"Mr. Schmid," she said loudly. "I'm sorry to disturb you." Though she waited for an answer, he didn't move. "Mr. Schmid," she said again, raising her voice as she took a step closer. "Are you asleep?"

His hand was on the computer mouse, but now she could see that his head was on the keyboard. It would be almost impossible to sleep like that. A bolt of fear shot down her spine.

She grasped him by the shoulder and

shook him. "Mr. Schmid," she said loudly. "Can you hear me?"

His head lolled around, pressing the keys on the keyboard.

Grasping him by both shoulders, and with a giant heave fueled by alarm, she pulled him away from the desk and back into the office chair. His head flopped against its back, where it came to a rest. Now that she could see his face, there was no mistaking his fate. His slack mouth was open and his lifeless and half-lidded eyes stared past her.

Rudy Schmid was dead.

18

Maris stood with Guy and Mac as the familiar scene unfolded. While the coroner and his assistant rolled the gurney from the store to the waiting van outside, the forensics team passed him on their way in.

"Sheriff," Lucille said. Mac was back in the usual khaki pants, long-sleeved shirt, and tie of the sheriff's uniform. "Didn't expect to see you so soon." She nodded to Maris. "Or you, Maris."

"I found the body," Maris replied.

"Guy," Mac said. "Could you hang a 'Closed' sign on the front door?"

The sheriff had spoken to the few customers who'd been in the store at the time, before ushering them out. Guy was the only person left. But he seemed not to have heard, and was staring out the front window at the coroner's van.

"Guy?" Mac said again.

The hardware store employee blinked and then stared at him. "I'm sorry. What?"

Maris gave him a sympathetic look. He was likely in a bit of shock.

"If you hang a 'Closed' sign on the door," Mac said, "that'll keep customers out."

Guy nodded. "Oh sure, Sheriff, sure."

"When you're done, just wait here. We'll be right back." He looked at the senior investigator and her young assistant. "Let me show you where the office is. Maris can describe what she saw."

He led the way, followed by Lucille and Sefina. Maris brought up the rear.

"Does the coroner have any theories?" Lucille asked.

"It could very well be another case of botulism," Mac said.

"Another?" Sefina said. "But..."

Mac glanced over his shoulder. "I know. We found no traces at Ms. Castro's house."

"You didn't?" Maris asked. "Nothing?"

Sefina glanced back at her. "Right. Either

she cleaned her kitchen super well, or it didn't come from there."

Mac had put yellow police tape across the door in an 'X' but took it down to allow the investigators in. Already in their hazmat suits, they added face masks and gloves before proceeding in.

"Where was the body?" Lucille asked.

"He was sitting in that chair but slumped on top of the desk," Maris said, pointing from the hallway. There was no way the office would hold more than two people—and she was glad to wait outside. "His head was on the keyboard."

While Sefina unpacked some supplies, Lucille looked at Maris. "Why did you come in here?"

Maris cleared her throat. "I was, um, looking for the restroom. I opened the door and found him on the desk."

Lucille exchanged a look with Mac who pointedly looked at the 'Office' sign on the door, and then at the 'Restroom' sign on the opposite door, before returning his gaze to Maris.

"I didn't touch anything," Maris continued. "Just Rudy. I thought perhaps he was napping, but then he didn't respond. I was worried and pulled him back from the desk."

"All right," Lucille said, and turned back to Sefina. "Let's get out the evidence markers."

"We'll leave you to the crime scene," the sheriff said.

"Crime scene," Maris said lowly as they turned away.

"Right," Mac said. "I can't afford to take chances. We might have a serial poisoner on our hands."

They headed back up the hallway. "Then Joy might have been murdered," Maris said.

As they made their way into the lighting aisle, Mac said, "I have to entertain that possibility now."

They found Guy at the cash register, putting the cash in a zippered money bag. He looked up as they approached. "Closing out the till," he said, his face glum. "Normally Rudy would do this."

Mac took the notepad from his pocket. "When was the last time you saw Mr. Schmid?"

Guy paused and put the money bag on the counter. He looked up at the round clock above the front door. I'd say a couple of hours ago. Maybe about nine o'clock."

Mac nodded. "And where was he?"

Guy blinked and looked down at his feet. "Right here." He stared at the cash register. "He was ringing up a customer. I went to help someone find the right nails in the hardware aisle."

"How did he seem?" Maris asked.

The store employee shrugged his big shoulders. "Same as always." He grimaced and shook his head. "I wish I'd known. Maybe I could have done something." He looked at Maris and then Mac. "What did he die of?"

"We won't know until the autopsy report is back," Mac said.

Guy tugged on his red soul patch, his eyes cast down. "I wish I'd known something was wrong." He grimaced and shook his head. "I'd have done anything for the man."

"Were you close?" Maris asked.

He looked up at her. "Not really, but Rudy was the only one willing to take a chance on me."

"When were you released?" Mac asked.

Maris frowned and cocked her head at

him, but Guy immediately said, "Almost a year ago now." He smiled a little at Maris. "Cops always know."

Her brows drew together as she looked between the two men. "Know what?"

"I was in prison," Guy said. He gazed at Mac. "It's the tattoos, isn't it?"

Maris stared at the scripted tattoos on his neck, but couldn't make out what they read.

Mac gave him an appraising look. "The tattoos, the shaved head." He jutted his chin toward Guy's arm. "The time you spent in the workout yard."

The young man bunched his hand and flexed his bicep under the baggy shirt. "It's either that or–"

"Or be a victim," Mac said.

"Dog eat dog," Guy agreed. "It's not the guards you worry about." He glanced at Maris. "It's the other cons."

Mac made a note in his pad. "What were you in for?"

"Stupidity," Guy said with a chuckle. But when Mac looked up from the notepad, he stifled the laugh. "I sold pot and got six months."

Mac nodded. "And how long have you been working here?"

Guy tugged on his soul patch again. "I'm not sure. Maybe nine months?"

Maris did the math. "It took you three months to find a job?"

"A decent paying one," Guy said. "I didn't do much time, but no real business wanted to hire me." He grimaced and looked at the cash register. "Until Rudy."

There was a knock at the front door. All three of them looked over to see Heather Schmid through the glass. She banged on it with the flat of her hand. "Let me in."

19

―――――

"Mrs. Schmid," Guy said, as he opened the door, "what are you doing here?"

"I heard that police cars were still here," she said. "I want to know what's going on."

Maris had never met Heather Schmid, but up close she was struck by the older woman's beauty. Her straight, white hair was cut in a cute bob, with bangs straight across her forehead. She was trim and apparently prematurely gray, since Maris would have put her age at around the mid-fifties. In fact the more she looked at Heather, the more she realized she'd likely been exceptionally pretty in her youth. Her aquamarine eyes darted from Guy to Maris and then finally Mac.

"As I said on the phone, Mrs. Schmid,"

the sheriff said, "our investigation is ongoing." He smiled at her. "I know this has to be a difficult time. There's no need for you–"

"My husband is dead, Sheriff," she said. "I need to know what's happening." She glanced at Maris but then focused on Mac again. "If Rudy was in the hospital, I'd be there. But he's not." She swallowed hard. "So I'm here, and I think I have a right to know what's happening here."

Mac returned her gaze and then nodded. "All right, Mrs. Schmid." He indicated the patio and outdoor section with his notepad. "Why don't we go over here and have a seat." He looked at Guy. "If you'll finish up with the till..."

"Okay," he said, and went back to the cash register.

Maris pointed to the small refrigerated unit at the end of the counter. "I'll just bring some water."

"Good," Mac said. "Thanks."

As the sheriff led Heather to the small arrangement of plastic patio furniture, Maris grabbed a few bottles of cold water. When she joined them, Mac was explaining what the forensics team was doing. Maris opened one of the bottles and set it in front of Heather, who immediately took a drink.

As Maris took a seat, she said, "We haven't met, but I'm Maris Seaver."

"Maris found your husband's body," the sheriff added. "I asked her to remain here to give forensics all the details."

"Oh," Heather said, and put the bottle down, staring at it. "I see." Finally she looked up at Maris. "Thank you. I'm sure that must have been..." A pained expression crossed Heather's face.

"I thought maybe I could help him," Maris said truthfully, while omitting the precognitive vision that had prompted her visit.

Heather's eyes looked all over Maris's face. "I...I appreciate that you tried."

"Mrs. Schmid," the sheriff said, "when was the last time you saw your husband?"

"When he left for work this morning," she answered, her voice more sure. "Right after breakfast, like always, at six thirty."

"Do you remember what he ate?" Mac asked, as he made a note.

"Same thing he always had. Three eggs, rye toast, and four links of sausage."

As Mac noted all of that down, Maris had

no doubt he was thinking the same thing that she was: had there been anything that might have fostered the growth of the *Clostridium botulinum* bacteria—and more importantly, its toxin?

"Coffee?" Mac asked.

"Yes," Heather replied. "Always coffee, and he took a cup in his travel mug too." She glanced at the back of the store and deflated a little. "Oh, I guess I'll have to figure out how to get his truck home."

"I'd like to take a look at it first," the sheriff said. When she turned back to him, he added, "Just to be complete. Then I can have it delivered to your home."

She nodded slightly. "Thank you."

He set his notepad and pen on the glass tabletop. "How long were you and Mr. Schmid married?"

A wistful smile softened her features. "Next month it would have been thirty-five years."

Maris arched her brows. "Goodness. You must have gotten married as a child."

Heather shook her head, her smile evaporating. "We met in college and married very quickly." She looked down at her wedding and engagement rings. The pear-shaped diamond was a large solitaire. "I quit my degree to take care of the home." A brief look of embarrassment crossed her face as she glanced at Maris. "I know it sounds ridiculously old fashioned, but he took care of me, and I took care of the house and everything that entails. I've never worked outside the home."

"There's nothing wrong with old fashioned," Maris told her, smiling. "Honestly, when you put it like that, it sounds positively romantic."

"Mrs. Schmid," the sheriff said, "I want you to think carefully about this next question, and take your time." Both she and Maris looked at him. "Are you aware of anyone who might want to see harm come to your husband?"

Heather made a derisive sound and frowned. "Every woman who ever came in the store."

Maris's mouth dropped open but she quickly shut it.

"I see," Mac said, picking up the notepad again. "Anyone in particular?"

"No," she said simply. "I wish I could tell you, but I was hardly here." She paused and turned to look at the front of the store. "The only person who I ever saw was that woman in the plaza on picnic day."

"Joy Castro," Maris said, looking out at the Towne Plaza. She could see the place where Joy had died.

Heather turned back to look at them. "I never knew her name."

"So you say you were hardly here," the sheriff said, "and yet you say every woman who ever came in would have wanted to see harm come to your husband."

"He was a bully to women," she said bluntly. "I witnessed it many times, even his own mother." Her earnest look took them both in. "But never me," she said firmly. "Not once. He was always different with me."

Rudy Schmid was sounding decidedly less romantic with every little bit that Maris learned.

"All right," Mac said, noncommittally.

"Honestly," Heather said, "the love had gone out of our marriage long ago, but there was always the partnership. He relied on me and I relied on him. He never once let me down, and I always stood by him."

"And where were you this morning?" the

sheriff asked.

"At home," she said, "like most days, unless I have to shop."

At that moment, Guy returned with the money bag and put it on the patio table. "I'm not sure where this is supposed to go. I always gave it to Rudy."

Heather stared at it, but said nothing.

"Is there a safe?" Mac asked standing.

"I don't know," Guy answered, tugging on his soul patch. "I never went in the office. There might be one in there."

As Heather got to her feet, Mac helped her and pulled out her chair, and Maris discreetly tapped her temple.

"There was no safe in the office that I could see," Maris said, standing as well.

Mac picked up the cash bag and held it out to Heather. "Then I suggest you keep it, Mrs. Schmid."

"Me?" she said, almost recoiling from it. "But I...I never handled the money."

Maris lightly touched the other woman's shoulder. "I think you might have to start," she said gently.

Heather stared down at the bag. "Oh," she said, and tentatively took it from Mac.

"I'd like the shop to stay closed for the rest of the day," he told both her and Guy. He fished in his breast pocket for some business cards and handed them each one. "If there's anything else that either of you remember, please call me." Both Guy and Heather took the cards and glanced at them.

Guy tucked it into his pants pocket. "Can we open tomorrow?"

"It depends on whether or not forensics is finished," Mac said.

The hardware store employee frowned. "Rudy would have wanted it to stay open." Although Heather regarded the young man, she didn't say anything.

"I'm sure that's true," Mac said. "But the investigators need to finish their work." He paused for a second, and then said, "Is there a spare key for the doors?"

Guy immediately removed a set that had been clipped to his belt loop. "I have one," he said, taking it from the ring. "The front and back use the same one." He placed it in the sheriff's outstretched palm.

"Thanks," Mac said. "I'll lock up today and give you a call later to let you know about tomorrow."

20

Mac locked the front door behind Guy and Heather when they left, giving them both a little nod through the glass. He adjusted the 'Closed' sign so that it hung straight, and then turned to Maris. Subconsciously she'd crossed her arms over her chest as she'd watched them depart.

"Right," Mac said. "Your body language is showing what I'm thinking. None of this is making sense."

"To say the least," Maris agreed, and then had an idea. "Let's start from the beginning." She gazed around their vicinity. "First, Joy Castro has an argument with Rudy Schmid on the morning of picnic day. Here. He refuses service to her and she leaves."

"Then," the sheriff said, "she sees him and Heather at the picnic, and gives him a piece of her mind."

"At that point," Maris said, "she's already been poisoned by the salsa."

Mac nodded. "She dies at the picnic, and it seems like a case of food poisoning."

"But now," Maris said, looking to the back of the store, "two days later, Rudy dies."

"And it seems likely due to the same cause," Mac noted.

"But how?" Maris said, throwing out her hands. "How could the two cases of food poisoning be connected?"

Mac paused for a moment, but then said, "The only connection between the two victims is their arguments—the only *apparent* connection."

Heather and Guy had both got in different cars and were now gone. "Heather says she'd never met Joy, but what if that wasn't true?" She thought for a moment, and then shook her head. "Even so, what would be her motive to see Joy dead?"

"She said that she stood by her husband," Mac mused, "but I wouldn't exactly call that motive."

Maris nodded. "And she admits that the love had gone out of their marriage, but that's not a motive for murder either."

"Although," Mac interjected, "she doesn't seem overly distraught at her husband's death."

Maris gazed out the window again. "No. She doesn't."

Approaching footsteps caused them both to look toward the aisles. Lucille was in the lead and carrying an armful of evidence bags. She'd lowered her face mask. "We need to make one more trip for the gear boxes," she said to Mac. He quickly went to the door and opened it for Sefina, who was also carrying several evidence bags, but Lucille paused. "We're done collecting evidence though."

Maris looked at the various bags the senior investigator held. Rudy had apparently brought his lunch from home in an actual lunch box. They had also collected the travel mug that Heather had mentioned. They must have gone through the desk as well, since Maris hadn't seen the pack of gum, container of breath mints, or the chapstick in the office. They'd been very thorough.

"All right," Mac said. "Thanks for the

quick work. Are you done with the crime scene?"

Lucille nodded. "You can have it."

Sefina came back in and passed them, heading to the back.

"Was there anything that jumped out at you?" Mac asked, eying the collection of bags.

Lucille took them to the counter and picked one up. The plastic bag held a large plastic jar, and in it was a large syringe with a downturned needle. Maris arched her eyebrows.

"Was the victim on any medications?" the investigator asked.

Mac shook his head. "I don't know, but I'm going to be finding out." But then he took a second look at the evidence. "This isn't a piece of medical equipment. It's the type of syringe used for epoxy."

Maris cocked her head at it, but Lucille shook the jar a bit. "I don't think that's epoxy," she said.

"No," Mac said, looking closer. "It's not viscous enough. You're right." He looked at Lucille. "Good call."

Sefina brought three gear boxes through.

"That's everything," the young woman said, and headed outside.

Lucille gathered up the bags again. "I'll let you know if we find anything," she said, heading toward the door. "We'll start testing right away."

"Thanks, Lucille," Mac said, following her to the door. As she exited, he held the door for Maris. Once they were outside and he'd locked it, he turned to her.

"What's your next step?" Maris asked.

"I'm going to have to start looking for some other connection between the two victims," he said. "Just regular old shoe leather, I'm afraid."

Since Joy had lived in Cheeseman Village, there'd be some ground to cover. "Is there anything that I can do?" she asked.

Mac shook his head but smiled. "I'll take it from here, but thanks for your help today."

Maris had to grimace a little. "I wish I could say it was my pleasure."

21

Maris was on her way to her car when she noticed Max peeking out the front window of his pizzeria. He darted to the door as she approached.

As he opened it, he cupped his mouth. "Pssst, *Bella*," he whispered. He beckoned her inside with a quick motion, even as he checked right and left on the sidewalk.

"Max," she said, coming inside. He shut the door behind her. "What's up?"

"I was about to ask you the same thing," he said. "I saw Heather and Guy leave. They both looked upset. Has something happened to Rudy?"

Word was likely already out and spreading in the small town. Everyone had seen what Max had, and the emergency vehicles.

"I'm afraid so," she said. "Rudy Schmid is dead. I found his body this morning in his office."

Max's eyes grew huge. "*You?*" He shook his head as if to clear it. "*Found his body?*" He put a hand to his forehead. "*No.*" His face had gone white.

"Here," Maris said, guiding him to one of the stools next to the shelf table. "Have a seat."

As she put her purse down, the Italian chef slumped onto the stool. When she sat as well, he peered into her face. "Are you all right?"

Maris gave him a little smile. "I'm fine." The real shock had come with the precognitive vision. Actually finding the store owner dead had been more like the other shoe dropping. But when Max continued to stare at her, she added, "Really. I'm totally fine."

"Okay," he said nodding. "Okay." He stared at the wall as though he could see through it to the hardware store. "What happened to him?"

Maris tilted her head to the side and

scowled. "I'm afraid we won't know for sure until the coroner is done."

With a stern look that furrowed his eyebrows and brought attention to his crooked nose, he said, "What do *you* think happened?"

Maris considered for a moment, before offering an observation. "I'd have to say that Rudy and Joy might possibly have shared the same fate."

"Oh no," Max muttered, shaking his head. Suddenly he sat bolt upright. "Did he have my pizza?"

"Your pizza?" Maris asked, recalling the lunchbox. "No, not that I saw. What would make you think he had your pizza?"

"Guy, his employee, had come in for one," Max said. "Earlier today."

"Really," Maris said. There'd been no sign of any other food at all.

"Yes," Max said, nodding his head once. "He comes in almost every day." He managed a lopsided smile. "And I can tell you that I appreciate that vote of confidence. Especially with the grand opening only a few days away." He paused and his smile slipped. "Especially   with...everything   that   has happened."

Maris nodded. "I'm sure the coroner will have this cleared up quickly. Sooner than the grand opening."

"Of course," Max said, though he didn't sound at all encouraged.

Although Maris wished there was something she could do to allay the restauranteur's fears, the only thing she could really do was get to the bottom of the two deaths—possibly murders.

Max lightly thumped his hand down on the table. "I can only do what I can do," he declared. Then he stood. "I will cook."

Maris smiled at him as she stood too, and took her purse. She could imagine Cookie doing the same thing. "That's a great plan. Keep busy."

Max put the stools back in place. "*Precisamente*. Time will fly." He turned to head to the kitchen, but paused and gave her a grateful look. "*Grazie, Bella*."

"You're welcome, Max. *Ciao*."

22

Finally back at the B&B, much later than she'd planned, Maris went straight through to the back, exiting onto the side porch. As expected, Cookie was in her garden, but put down the potted plant she held as soon as she saw Maris.

"What happened?" the chef asked, coming over to the border where Maris joined her.

"Rudy Schmid died this morning," she said without preamble. "It looks like it could be another case of botulism."

"You're kidding," Cookie said, her gloved hands dropping to her sides. "Another?"

Maris grimaced. "That's what it looked like."

"But how in the world could..." Understanding dawned on the chef's face. She narrowed her eyes. "Murder?"

With a reluctant nod, Maris said, "That's the way Mac is going to treat them."

"Them," Cookie repeated. "Joy Castro and Rudy Schmid." She put her gloved fists on her hips. "An unlikely pair if ever there was one."

"I completely agree," Maris said. "I can't see how they'd possibly be connected."

At that moment, a loud and familiar meow sounded from the porch's screen door. Both women looked over to see Mojo's big eyes staring at them. The orange orbs disappeared when his eyes closed as he meowed again. Then he turned and bounced away.

Cookie chuckled a bit under her breath. "Maybe you're about to find out about their connection."

Maris smiled and turned on her heel. "Maybe."

Back in the library, Mojo was nowhere in sight. But as Maris went to the hallway, she saw him disappear into the parlor. It was going to be a Ouija clue. Except once she entered the parlor, she discovered that the Ouija board was gone.

"What?" Maris muttered. Mojo jumped up to the coffee table where it was usually displayed. "Where is it?" she asked, just as Mojo yowled. "Yeah," she told him. "Me too."

She turned in place scanning the room. To her relief, she spotted it immediately. It'd been tucked on top of some books in the bookshelf. As she went to retrieve it, she frowned a little. Neither she nor Cookie put it anywhere but on the table. Maybe one of the guests had used it and then stowed it away.

As she brought it over, Mojo watched intently and gave her his tiny, tinny meow.

"I know," she said. "I'm moving as fast as I can." She held the board and planchette out in front of her. "You know, it'd help if you weren't in the way."

He quickly crossed the table and sat down at its end.

Surprised, Maris said, "Thank you."

No sooner did the board touch wood than Mojo was on top of it. Maris stood back.

"You're anxious today," she told him. Or maybe he'd been perturbed by the board not being in its rightful place.

But as she watched, he settled into position and immediately looked into the distance. He really wasn't wasting any time. Soon one ear began to spin and his gaze became fixed and unfocused. Then the other velvety ear began to cock one way and then the other. Without warning, his paw lifted and then landed on the planchette, moving it to the first letter.

"B," Maris whispered. The fuzzy black paw wasted no time in moving to the adjacent letter. "A," Maris said lowly. Without pausing, the planchette slid back to the middle of the board. Its plastic window hovered over the 'T.'

A bat? Maris thought. *Which kind? The animal or a piece of wood?*

But Mojo wasn't through. The planchette made a move she'd never seen before. It was heading toward the numbers at the bottom. This would be a first. But the planchette quickly stopped and went back to the 'T.'

Maris cocked her head down at it. He'd spelled a double T.

There was no time to ponder it, however, as the little black cat slid the planchette over to the 'E.'

"What in the world?" Maris muttered. BATTE?

In the next few seconds, though, she had her answer. Just under the 'E,' Mojo moved the planchette down over the 'R.' Then, with a long and skittering slide, finished with the 'Y.'

"Battery," Maris said. Mojo blinked and looked up at her. He gave her his signature meow. "Yeah," she said. "I see it. Battery." She picked him up and gave his head a gentle pat. "And you set a land speed record spelling it."

But as she stared down at the board, she had no idea what it could mean. Maybe the hardware store carried batteries.

"Or maybe it's a car battery?" she asked him. Maybe she ought to ask Jude over at Flour Power Sandwiches & Gas. "Is that it?"

Rather than give her an answer, he squirmed to be put down, and Maris obliged him. Without a backward glance, he bounced away, into the hallway, and disappeared.

"Thanks," she called out to him. But when she followed him out, he was gone. For a moment she paused and looked back at the board. He'd been awfully anxious to spell that word. She was going to have to track down something that had to do with batteries.

But as the late afternoon light cast long shadows across the Persian rug, Maris knew her search for the meaning of the clue would have to wait. It was time to get ready for the Wine Down.

23

The next morning after breakfast, Maris was intent on making up for lost time. Yesterday, following Rudy Schmid's death, most of the day had been spent in town. As she turned down the guest beds and dusted, Cookie made sure there were enough toiletries and fresh towels. Although they passed each other on the stairs and in the hallways, Maris found herself lost in thought.

It seemed clear now why Claribel had shown her the dingy little office. Unfortunately, Maris hadn't recognized it. If she had, then perhaps she could have done something to prevent Rudy's death. What was much less obvious were Mojo's clues: the seven of swords and a battery. Even more obscure was what would link Rudy with Joy, and mean they had to be killed.

"Who would stand to benefit?" Maris muttered.

Guy had been more upset than Heather at her husband's death. If Superior Hardware went out of business, he'd have no job. If anything, he had a vested interest in seeing Rudy alive and well.

When the dryer sounded, Maris trotted down the stairs, dusting the banister as she went. She'd found that if she were prompt with the machine loads, she could cut the washing and drying time by almost a half hour. Once the next loads were running, she began folding the linens—the napkins and matching tablecloth from the dining room.

Again, her thoughts returned to yesterday. Heather had not seemed overwrought with sadness and been frank about the state of her marriage. Like Guy, she seemed to have a vested interest in seeing her husband alive, having never worked outside the home.

Maris paused.

"But what about a life insurance policy?" she murmured.

Had Rudy been the type to make sure his

wife would be taken care of, in the event of his death? For a moment she wondered if Mac would be looking at that possibility, but then nodded to herself. Of course he would. After her aunt's death, he'd asked much the same questions of her.

As she opened the linen cabinet, she suddenly thought of Max. After Bear had repaired his oven, he'd joked about making his restaurant wider. The pizzeria was indeed an incredibly narrow place, probably contributing to it having been vacant. But could the big-hearted Italian chef have the type of ambition for his restaurant that he'd actually kill someone. More than once he'd asked about his pizza in connection with the deaths.

Could there actually be a link?

Cookie had already posited that he was one of the magick folk, with a talent like hers but with food and not potions. Surely he'd use his magic ability rather than botulism to kill someone.

A shiver ran down her spine.

If anyone were capable of food poisoning, wouldn't it be someone whose magic ability involved food?

"Are you hanging on to the knobs for any particular reason?" Cookie asked. She put a load of dish towels on top of the washing machine.

Startled out of her thoughts, Maris realized she'd opened the doors to put away the linens but hadn't. "Just thinking," she said, as she quickly grabbed the linens and put them away.

"Well," Cookie said, "before you close that, you might want to take the duster out."

"What?" Maris said, yanking the doors back open. She'd set the napkins on top of it. "Oh, sorry." She snatched them out, along with the duster. When she turned the stack over to see the bottom napkin, she saw that she'd gotten it dirty. "I'll wash this one again," she said, peeling it off.

"You can toss it in with the dish towels," the chef said, standing aside. As they swapped places, Cookie took the clean napkins but didn't put them away. Instead, she unfolded them.

"What are you doing?" Maris asked, cocking her head at the older woman. "Are they dirty?"

"No," the older woman said, but she showed her one. "They're folded inside out."

"Oh for goodness sake," Maris said. "How did that happen?" She reached for one, but Cookie scooted them out of reach.

When she eyed the chef, the diminutive woman smiled placidly at her. "How did it happen?" She started to refold the napkins. "I think they call it multitasking."

Maris opened her mouth to protest, and then thought better of it. She could hardly argue with the fact that she'd been about to lose the duster—and probably spend fifteen minutes looking for it. But it hadn't been the multitasking, she'd been thinking about the murders.

"It's a lot to think about," Cookie said. "I know. But it doesn't help to be in a rush, or try to get three things done at once."

Maris stared at the older woman. If she hadn't already known that the chef was skilled with potions, she'd have said she was a mind-reader.

As Cookie took her time refolding the napkins, she glanced at Maris. "Do yourself a favor, my friend, and slow down. We only have three guests at the moment, and low maintenance ones at that. It's good to slow down."

Though she'd progressed in the battle to tame her Type A+ personality, she had to admit that she occasionally fell off the wagon. Even so, what was the harm in trying to be efficient? Could she help it if there'd been two murders in almost as many days? It was enough to keep anyone distracted.

But Maris sighed. After enough discussions like this, she knew better than to argue.

"Maybe I'll go finish cleaning the fresnel lens," Maris suggested.

Cookie regarded her. "More work?"

"I suppose you could call it that," she admitted, "but it's slow, quiet, and relaxing." As Cookie seemed to consider it, Maris added, "Maybe not unlike gardening. It seems to me that you spend a goodly amount of labor to provide the B&B with fresh herbs and beautiful flowers."

"Touché," the chef said, as she put away the napkins. She smiled as she turned back. "Have a nice time."

24

As Maris stood and backed up a pace, she surveyed her work. The Old Girl was positively glittering. With the morning fog burned off, sunshine flooded the optics house, turning the fresnel lens into a cascade of twinkles.

"So this is what it feels like," she said, smiling to herself.

For months she'd watched Bear start and complete projects, never seeming to rush. Likewise Cookie always seemed to be puttering in her garden, and yet new plants were always growing. Now she'd started and finished her own piece of work, taking her time and paying attention to the details. To say that it was satisfying didn't even come close. There was a deep sense of accomplishment and she was already looking forward to the next task.

For a few moments she walked around it, taking it all in, before looking out to the bay. She'd never really noticed how the water reflected the wispy clouds above. It turned the waves a dusty blue, a color that also seemed to be refracting through the lens. All of the elements played together, creating a tranquil space that was not simply a coincidence. She had no doubt that if she were here in the evening, the violet and orange hues would combine into something just as pretty and peaceful.

Maris felt the footsteps before she heard them. Someone was coming up the spiral staircase. But it wasn't Bear. Though nimble for a big man, his footfall was still heavy. No, whoever was climbing up was definitely lighter. Then she heard the voices.

"Look, sweetie," a young man's voice said. "There's a view through that window."

Maris smiled. It was the Yangs. She took off her nitrile gloves, and bent to pick up the used microfiber cloths.

"Oh I see it," Melanie said, her voice drawing closer.

In another few moments, Andrew appeared and stepped up to the landing. "Wow," he said, when he saw the view. He waited for his wife and took her hand as she stepped up.

"Wow," she whispered. "What a view."

Andrew glanced at Maris. "I hope we're not disturbing you."

"Not at all," Maris said.

"Look," Melanie said, pointing south. "There's the pier." She looked back at her husband. "We should go visit that, sweetie."

Maris, still carrying her cleaning cloths, came to the railing. "It's a beautiful pier and kept in its historic condition. At the end of the day, the local fisherman process their catch in the warehouse on the far end."

"That'd be interesting to see," Melanie said.

"And even better to taste," Andrew added.

Maris nodded out at the ocean beyond the bay. "If you've had any seafood locally, then you've already tasted it."

"Oh really," the optometrist said, turning to her. "That's actually one of the reasons we came up here when we saw you."

"We were wondering," Melanie said,

coming to his side, "if you could recommend a restaurant."

"Absolutely," Maris said. "Are you looking for a particular kind of cuisine or ambiance?"

"We're in the mood for something spicy," Andrew said. "Something with a little kick."

Maris nodded. "Then I can highly recommend Delia's Smokehouse, on the Towne Plaza."

"A smokehouse?" Melanie said, frowning. "You mean barbecue?"

With a little grin, Maris shook her head. "I mean the most amazing Shrimp Po' Boys or crab salads or smoked salmon you've ever had. You can specify your heat level or use their signature hot sauces, but beware 'Delia's Scorching Smokehouse.' You have been warned."

Andrew beamed back at her. "Duly noted." He turned to Melanie and arched his eyebrows at her.

She hugged him to her side. "Sounds good."

He gave her a little peck on the forehead.

Young love, Maris thought, smiling.

Andrew turned his attention back to her. "And now to the second reason. You said the other day that you were cleaning the optics. I thought we might be able to watch for a bit." He adjusted his glasses. "You might say I have a natural interest in glass of all kinds."

"And I teach science," Melanie said. "This will fascinate the kids."

Maris lifted the dusty cloths. "Well, I'm afraid I've just finished, but I'd be glad to talk you through the process."

As Bear had done with her, she listed the do's and don'ts, demonstrated the technique, and explained the rationale.

"Forget about the kids," Melanie said. "This is absolutely fascinating." The young woman grinned at Maris. "And who doesn't love lighthouses?"

Maris laughed a little. "You are preaching to the lightkeeper on that one."

"Thanks so much for showing us all that," Andrew said. "I'll have a completely new appreciation for the fresnel lens every time I see a lighthouse now." He gazed at his wife. "Shall we head to the smokehouse?"

She nodded. "I'm starving."

As they began their descent, Maris picked up the discarded gloves and dust cloths again. It was too bad the young couple hadn't wanted Italian food. She would have adored sending them to the pizzeria. Although it might be possible to stretch a point in order to find a motive for Max as far as Rudy's death, she simply couldn't believe he was capable of murder—let alone by poisoning someone's food. She'd no more expect it of him than she would of Cookie.

At the thought, Maris paused. It suddenly occurred to her how she might be able to help the pizzeria's grand opening. It would just take a few visits to get everything arranged.

While she descended the iron staircase, her mind moved from Max, the pizza, and the opening to the topic of botulism. She'd taken on face value the fact that it was highly deadly. But in reality, she had no idea how it actually worked. By the time she reached ground level, a plan had begun to form in her mind. As long as she needed to make a few visits, she'd stop in at the medical clinic and have a talk with Jill Maxwell.

25

———

When Maris entered the Pixie Point Bay Medical Clinic, she was reminded of the pizzeria. It was as narrow a space as the Towne Plaza offered. But instead of rustic brick ovens and a giant cooktop, the interior of the medical facility was starkly modern, clean, and minimalist.

Dressed in blue scrubs and sitting behind the white counter of the small lobby, Jill Maxwell, Nurse Practitioner, looked much as she had when Dr. Rossi had still been the head of the clinic. Although she welcomed patients as she'd always done, now she was also their primary physician.

"Maris," Jill said. "Good afternoon. What can I do for you?"

"Hi, Jill," Maris said and strolled over to the counter. "I was hoping you might have time to tell me a little about botulism."

"Anything in particular?" she asked.

"Timing," Maris replied. "How long does it take for someone to show symptoms, once they been poisoned?"

The nurse tilted her head. "Well, to paraphrase Paracelsus, the dose makes the poison. Tiny amounts injected below the skin," she said, and pointed to her temple, where tiny wrinkles were just beginning, "is a cosmetic treatment. You've probably heard of Botox."

Maris blinked at her. "Good grief. I certainly have. Are you saying that Botox is made from botulinum toxin?"

Jill nodded. "It's a commercial strain, but yes. However, if botulinum toxin were injected into the bloodstream, death could result from mere nanograms. If you ingest it, a microgram." When Maris frowned, she added, "It'd weigh less than, say, an eyelash."

"Good grief," Maris said again. "An eyelash." She thought for a moment. "And if you got that kind of dose, how long would it take for symptoms to appear?"

"It's difficult to say," Jill said. "But it could be as long as three days." She held up a finger. "But here is where Paracelsus comes in. If you were to get a massive dose, it wouldn't be three days but more like three hours."

"Okay," Maris said, "three hours to three days."

"Maybe even longer for minuscule doses," Jill said. "And let me be clear, it's not the bacteria that's poisonous, it's the neurotoxic protein that it creates. In other words, it stops nerve signal and creates paralysis." Maris recalled both Joy and Rudy's drooping eyelids. "Why the renewed interest?" the nurse asked. "Are you worried about something in particular? Because although the bacteria is present pretty much everywhere, it's easily managed with proper food preparation and storage techniques."

Maris paused for a few moments, but finally said, "It's likely that Rudy Schmid died of it."

"Ah," Jill said, looking out the clinic's front window. "I saw the commotion at the hardware store and heard that Rudy had died, but not of what."

"It's not widely known," Maris said, "and I

hasten to add that it hasn't yet been confirmed. Did you know Rudy?"

The nurse shook her head. "Not at all, but
I do know Heather. Poor thing. This is going
to be hard for her. They didn't have kids."

Though the death of a spouse was always
going to be hard, Maris sensed something
more than that—particularly since Heather
hadn't seemed racked with sorrow.

"You mean all the arrangements to be
made now?"

Jill frowned a little. "Well, there is that
too. But I was referring to their rather 'dated'
lifestyle. Heather bakes, cans, gardens,
cleans, sews... Well, she does everything in
terms of keeping a home. How she'll get by
outside the house, it's hard to imagine."

"You're right," Maris said. "That is going
to be tough." The front door of the clinic
opened and a middle-aged couple entered.
"Well, I won't keep you any longer. Thanks
very much for all that information."

"Any time," Jill said. Maris headed toward
the door, passing the couple. "Mr. and Mrs.
Hill, please come in."

Maris let the door close behind her, then
struck out across the grass toward Delia's

Smokehouse and her first request. But just before she reached it, she had to pause when something Jill said finally came to the forefront of her mind. She'd said that Heather canned.

26

Home for the evening, but without guests for the Wine Down, Maris sat with Cookie in the kitchen at the big butcher block. The chef had put together a simple Greek salad and also baked two generous portions of salmon. Maris gingerly opened their foil coverings to reveal the perfectly moist fish, topped with thin lemon slices and plenty of dill.

"This smells amazing," she said.

"Just something light and easy," Cookie said, as she served the salad.

For a few minutes, they simply ate in companionable silence. The lettuce, avocado, cucumber, red onions, Kalamata olives and feta cheese had just the right amount of tangy vinaigrette.

A little harmonica-like meow came from under the butcher block. Maris ducked her head to look under it.

"Mojo," she said. "When did you come in?"

He gave her another meow and bounced over to his dish. He circled it once and then sat down next to it, his big orange eyes locked onto her.

Cookie chuckled. "It would seem it's dinner time for everyone."

Maris set her napkin aside as she stood. "So it would seem."

She took the container of smoked salmon from the refrigerator, separated a nice piece, and took it to his bowl. Mojo stood as she placed it down—and then pounced. Maris quickly yanked her hand away.

"Um, bon appétit," she said.

When she sat down at the butcher block again, Cookie said, "Move just a little more slowly next time, and you'll pull back a stump."

Maris laughed. "Maybe I should get a glove."

"Speaking of which, how goes the fresnel lens cleaning?"

"You know," Maris said, spearing an olive, avocado cube, and slice of red onion all at once, "I'm a little sad to be done."

Cookie regarded her. "But do you have to be done?" She ate a forkful of salmon and cucumber combined.

Maris shrugged a little. "Well, I suppose I could just keep cleaning it, maybe start back at the beginning. But knowing me, I'd wear the glass pieces down to just wafers."

"Or you could move on to something else," Cookie said. "Like I do in the garden."

"Oh?" Maris said, and popped the vegetables in her mouth.

"It's a cycle of sorts," the chef said. "Planting seeds, seeing them germinate, transplanting them, and harvesting. That's one cycle. But there are also different areas of the garden, and different plants in them that mature in different seasons. There's always something new to keep me busy."

Maris considered that. Certainly Bear's list of maintenance chores for the optics house had been lengthy. But would any of those tasks prove as enjoyable? But the more she thought of Bear going about his jobs, the more she realized that he seemed to treat them all the same. Maybe it wasn't so much the job itself, but her attitude.

"You know what," Maris said smiling, "I'm going to talk to Bear about it."

"Good," Cookie said.

By the time they'd finished dinner, the sun had set. Though they couldn't see it, the lighthouse's beam would be turning up above. The house was so quiet that the distant sound of the surf on the rocks below the point could be heard.

Finished with her meal, Cookie got up and took her plate to the sink.

"Nope," Maris said, also finished and following her. "I'm on kitchen patrol tonight. You did the cooking."

Without missing a beat, Cookie said, "Fine by me. I was looking at that new coffee table book. I think that might be some good reading material for tonight."

"*The Secret Life of Redwoods?*" Maris asked, turning on the tap.

"Yes, that's the one," Cookie said. Maris watched her fetch her unfinished tea, and head to the doorway. The diminutive chef glanced back over her shoulder. "You two have a nice night."

Mojo, who had been cleaning his face, stopped and gave a short little mew.

"Sweet dreams," Maris said. "See you tomorrow."

As she rinsed the plates and utensils and put them in the dishwasher, Mojo circled around her ankles. "What should we do tonight?" she asked him.

Although he gave her no answer, he stopped his circling and looked up at her. It wasn't often that they had the evening to themselves. But then a thought occurred to her. She stowed the dish towel, reached down to his face, and gave his nose a light little boop. "Follow me, young man."

27

In her bedroom, Maris took the black skeleton key from its hook next to the door. The last time she'd searched for her aunt's missing pendulum, she'd found its ornate silver chain. In the interim, she'd convinced herself that the beautiful green stone that had once hung from it couldn't be far behind.

She'd also been making good progress with venturing farther into the enclosed basement. The mild claustrophobia that had been brought on by being trapped in an elevator was gradually easing. While her photographic memory almost always worked in her favor, it turned out that unpleasant experiences were sometimes remembered better than nice ones. Although Maris suspected that she'd never be completely free of anxiety when it came to being in confined spaces, she felt good about what she'd achieved so far.

Mojo trotted past her, through the bedroom to the far door—the one that led to the utility room that connected the lightkeeper's house with the lighthouse. It was also the only way to access the basement.

An impatient little mew told her that she was taking too long.

"I'm coming," she said.

On the floor of the utility room, the little black cat sat next to the door and was already peering at the massive black lock.

"Here we go," she said quietly, inserting the key into it.

The familiar grinding of the heavy gears greeted them. Mojo cocked his head one way and then the other as she continued to turn the key. But when the final clunk sounded, Mojo leapt back as though he'd been launched by a giant spring.

Maris jerked her hand back, as her heart leapt into her throat. "What?" she demanded, staring at the cat.

For a moment his big amber eyes stared at her. Then he looked back at the lock, with the key still protruding from it. As though it had given him a shock, he tentatively sniffed the wood floor next to it. Maris watched as he got closer to it, still sniffing, and then drew back.

"What?" she said, more quietly this time.

One of his ears jiggled, then the other, until he shook his entire head. When he'd finished, he simply walked to the wooden hatch and put his paw on it.

"Oh," Maris said, finally taking the key. "So, now you're ready? Now that you've given me a fright?"

Grasping the big black handle, she lifted the door and set it aside. Normally Mojo would rush right down, but tonight he simply peered into the darkness.

"All right," she said, taking a few steps down. "Now you're weirding me out. Are you in or not?"

She reached under the floor and flicked on the basement's fluorescent lights. But not even that tempted him. Instead, he reached out a paw to her.

"What is going on?" she said reaching for him. When she picked him up, he purred. "When did you get to be so skittish about a basement search?" He was starting to act like her.

Even as she thought it, she paused.

Had something happened to him recently that made him worried about the basement —maybe even having been trapped somewhere? As she stroked his head, she went down a few more steps. When he didn't seem to be bothered, she went down a few more.

"All right," she told him, "we'll do this together."

On the left, they passed the diagonal collection of books that had been her first introduction to what lay in store below. At the bottom of the steps were the familiar hat boxes, and off to the side the dresser with the old suitcase on top. She had searched the dresser drawers completely when she'd found the silver chain, so she passed it up. But as she neared the edge of known territory, a familiar tightness in her chest began. Whether Mojo sensed it or not, she didn't know, but he chose that moment to look up at her. Then he squirmed to be put down.

"Have it your way," she said, as he bounced lightly away.

They ended up near two large crates against the wall. He jumped up on the first, and then the second, at her eye level. Though she glanced back over her shoulder to the stairs and felt the perspiration on her forehead, she was determined to at least make a little search now that she was here.

When she glanced back at Mojo, he'd turned toward the wall and was sniffing it.

"What could be interesting about a wall?" she muttered.

But as she watched him slowly move sideways to keep exploring, she realized it wasn't a wall.

"A door?" she said, her eyes widening.

Though the wood had faded to gray, as had its frame, it was definitely a door. It was made even easier to miss by its edges, hidden by a thick layer of dust. It looked like it hadn't been opened for many years—understandable with the big wooden shipping crates in front of it. But if it was a door...

"The basement could be huge," she whispered.

With a quick look at her surroundings,

and knowing the layout of the house above, she guessed that they were in the vicinity of her bedroom door. If that was the case, it was possible that the basement floor ran the entire length of the B&B.

"Good grief," she said as her mind tried to wrap itself around the new dimensions.

But having discovered the door, Mojo was no longer interested in it. Instead, he jumped down from the top crate and landed on a wood box to the side of it. But unlike the bottom crate on which it also sat, the wood was finished. In fact, the more Maris looked at it, the more she realized how nicely it was made. Its softly rounded corners were joined by fine mortised tenons. On top was a lid that looked about three inches deep, with an ornate brass handle. Two more handles were on either side, but they looked more like suitcase handles. The entire thing was about two feet on each side and now Maris could see that it had drawers all down its front.

Her pulse quickened. "Is this a jewelry box?" If there was anywhere she'd find the beautiful green stone pendulum, it'd be here.

Eagerly, she pulled out the top drawer,

but it wasn't jewelry that she found. It was a treasure of a completely different kind.

"Would you look at this," she muttered, picking up a tiny screwdriver with a wooden handle. She glanced at the other drawers. "It's a toolbox."

She returned the screwdriver to its rightful place, in order of height among the others. The next drawer seemed to contain measuring tools. She picked up what looked like a thick ruler with metal ends, but realized that it could be unfolded and might be used to measure up to a yard. Replacing it, she also saw a compass that still held a pencil, a small right angle, and a bubble level.

Mojo jumped down to the first crate, and sniffed the edge of the box.

All the drawers held similar collections of hand tools that must have once belonged to a fine craftsman. In fact, Maris didn't even recognize several of the tools. The last drawer at the bottom was the deepest and the heaviest. Mojo watched as she finally tugged it open. She barely had time to see something pink in the front corner of the drawer, before Mojo snatched it up.

"Hey," she protested, reaching for it. Only then did she see what it was—a toy mouse with little black beads for eyes and a thick string for a tail. "Oh," she said, as Mojo watched her. She smiled at him. "I might have known."

He leapt down from the crate and trotted back to the stairs.

Maris quickly closed the tool box. "So much for teamwork." Although she grasped the handles to either side and lifted, the box barely budged.

"Whoa," she said, letting them go. A wooden toolbox full of tools was heavy. She'd have to get Bear to help her.

She turned back to the stairs just in time to see Mojo race up them—without the toy. As she hurried to follow him, she glanced in every direction, but there was no sign of it. He'd somehow managed to stash it already.

He was waiting for her at the top of the stairs.

"You know," she told him as she lowered the hatch, "if we really are a team, you'd show me where the toys are."

Rather than mew, or purr, or even leave, he simply sat there and stared at her.

She regarded him in return. "I see." She locked the door and stood, looking down at him. "Well, next time we'll see who's a team player or not."

When she left, he was still sitting there.

28

___

The next morning, when Bear brought his empty breakfast tray in from the porch, Maris was waiting. She and Cookie had just finished loading the dishwasher after another praiseworthy meal. He set down the tray and the dishes were so clean that you'd never know there'd been a tall stack of pancakes, three muffin and egg sandwiches, and a small mountain of breakfast potatoes.

"Thank you, Cookie," he said. "It was delicious."

At the sink, ringing out a rag, she smiled at him over her shoulder. "You're very welcome, my young friend."

Maris took the tray to the sink. "Bear," she said, "before you start your work today, I wonder if you could help me with something."

"I will," he said.

Maris grinned at him as she rinsed his plates. "You haven't even heard what I'm going to ask."

He shrugged, and a little color rose to his cheeks. "I can always help. Everybody can."

As Maris loaded the dishes, she said, "Now that's a can-do attitude if I've ever heard one." She closed the dishwasher and dried her hands on a towel. "I found a vintage toolbox in the basement yesterday. I tried to lift it but it's too heavy."

He frowned a little. "You shouldn't lift heavy things, Maris."

As she passed him and headed toward the hallway, she waved her hand. "Oh believe me. I most certainly did not lift it. It's dead weight, as far as I'm concerned."

He followed her to her bedroom, but stopped at the door. When she grabbed the key and went to the opposite side of the room, she realized he hadn't followed her. When she looked back, he gave her an odd little wave.

"I'll go through the lighthouse," he said, and was gone.

"But..." she said, though it was too late. "It's faster this way," she said to no one. She shrugged. In the utility room, she unlocked and opened the hatch, just as Bear came through the door on the other side. "That was quick."

He was breathing a little hard, and just nodded his head.

"I'll show you where it is," she said.

On her way down the stairs, she turned on the lights. At the bottom, she stood aside and pointed toward the wooden shipping containers. "It's on top of that first crate."

Without a word, he went over to it, grasped the side handles, and lifted it. By the way he turned and walked back, it seemed like it weighed no more than a bag of groceries to him.

She quickly led the way back up. When he exited the way he'd come in, she closed and locked the hatch, before following him out. He was already halfway to the side porch by the time she left the lighthouse through its other door.

The fog had just started to lift as Maris

followed him to the table where they usually had lunch. He gently set it down and slowly ran his thick fingers over its rounded corners.

"This is nice," he said quietly.

"It's so nice," Maris told him, "that, at first, I thought it was a jewelry box."

He delicately took the ornate brass handle at the top, and opened the lid. Inside, as neatly arranged as the rest, were some small glass bottles and folded cloths.

"Do you think any of these would be useful?" she said.

His eyes got big. "Useful?" He pulled open the other drawers, one at a time, examining each with an appreciative murmur. He closed the last one. "All of them."

Maris frowned a little. "All of them? I mean, I don't even know what some of these things are." She picked up an odd metal tool from the top tray, where it had been stored with the bottles. "Like this."

When he held out his hand for it, she gave it to him.

"Especially this," he said. "It cuts glass."

She gawked at it. "That?"

About the size and shape of a pencil, it had a metal ball at one end as big as a marble. At the other end it was jagged, as though little u-shaped chunks of it had been sawed out.

Bear ran his finger over the tip of the jagged end. "This is a carbide wheel." When Maris took a closer look, she could see a tiny metal wheel at the very tip. "You dip it in oil." He pointed to the little bottles. After he switched his grip to hold the glass cutter like a pencil, he made as if he was drawing a straight line with it. "Then you score the glass." He flipped the tool around. "Use the ball to tap underneath the score so that the glass starts to crack. Then you just break it off. If there are jagged parts left on it, you can use these teeth." He thumbed the u-shaped cutouts. "The edge of the glass goes in these, depending on the thickness, and you can crack them off." He picked up one of the stoppered bottles and shook it next to his ear. "It still has oil."

"Wow," Maris said. "Tools to cut glass." She glanced up at the optics house. "Pretty handy to have at a lighthouse."

Bear put the cutter and bottle back. "This is a treasure," he said. "Especially with the hardware store closed."

"Closed?" Maris asked, recalling that Mac had locked up yesterday. "Still?"

The big man nodded. "It was this morning. I might have to start shopping in Cheeseman Village." He carefully closed the lid of the tool chest. "I shop there more now anyway, when Superior Hardware doesn't have what I need." He patted the top of the wood chest. "Should I put this away?"

"Back in the basement?" Maris asked.

He shook his head. "I was thinking in the garage, where it would be handy."

Maris smiled at him. "That would be great, Bear. Thanks."

29

Once her chores were done, Maris tracked down Cookie. Today would be an excellent day to pick up lunch, since she'd be visiting so many restaurants. She found the older woman doing an inventory of the pantry.

"Anything we need?" Maris asked her.

Cookie slid one of the clear drawers back into place. "Nothing at the moment," she said, glancing over her shoulder. "The guests really aren't spending a lot of time here."

When she turned to her, the older woman eyed the purse. "Heading into town?"

Maris nodded. "I've got several stops to make. Does any place in particular strike you as good for a lunch pickup?"

Cookie put a finger to her chin. "Let's

see." Maris could see the gears turning behind her eyes—likely pulling up an inventory of what they'd eaten recently. "Will you be stopping by Flour Power?"

"In fact, I will," Maris said.

"Wonderful," said the chef. "It's been a while since we've had any of Fab's subs."

Cookie headed to the door and Maris followed her, turning off the light. "Any sandwich in particular?"

"They're all good," Cookie said, as she went to the kitchen. She stopped and turned. "Why don't you pick?"

Maris smiled. "I think I can do that." She gave her a little wave. "See you in a bit."

Outside in the warm sun and briny breeze, Maris strode to her car. As she glanced at the garage, she thought of Bear putting the toolbox there. But then she remembered what he'd said about visiting the hardware store. As she got in and strapped on the seat belt, she remembered rushing there to find business as usual and Guy helping a customer who couldn't find something. As she started the engine, she recalled Max telling her that Bear had to improvise with the pizza oven. Then, when she'd first visited

Superior Hardware, she'd bought the last box of small nitrile gloves.

"Hmm," she muttered, and gently tapped her temple.

In her mind's eye she saw the scene in Rudy's office when she'd discovered his body. She focused on the computer screen. He'd been working on some type of ledger that looked like a list of the goods in the store. She'd seen similar types of reports in her years in the hospitality industry. It was a database summary, an inventory.

She frowned when she realized that many of the line items were highlighted in red.

Was Rudy having a cash flow problem?

Maris started the car. Even if he was, what did that have to do with someone poisoning him or Joy?

As Maris pulled through the driveway of Flour Power Gas & Sandwiches, she passed the red, 1950s style pumps and retro overhang to park in front of the shop. Next to it, the repair bay's rolling door was up and she could see Jude's legs sticking out from underneath someone's car. As she turned off the engine and dropped the keys in her purse, her phone rang. It was Mac.

"Good morning, Sheriff," she said, smiling.

"'Oh life, how pleasant in thy morning'," he said. "'Young Fancy's rays the hills adorning.'"

Maris had to grin. "Was Burns a morning person?"

Mac laughed. "Only when it came to poems. Old Rabbie was probably more of a drink-late-into-the-night kind of guy."

Maris chuckled. "I see. It's hard to get up in the wee hours, when you're up until the wee hours."

"Exactly," he agreed. "But as much as I'd like to talk all things Burns with you, I'm calling with some information."

"Great," Maris said. "I have something for you too."

"Good," he said. "The coroner's report has come back. Rudy Schmid did, in fact, die of botulism poisoning."

Though he couldn't see it, Maris nodded. "No surprise there."

"The surprise wasn't in his system," the sheriff said. "It was in his desk."

"A surprise?" she asked.

She heard the rustle of papers. "That large, plastic syringe was found in the middle drawer. It was loaded with botulinum toxin."

A shudder ran down her spine. "Good grief. An entire syringe full?"

"Exactly," he said. "It'd be enough to kill the entire county."

She frowned. "I guess you could call it a smoking syringe, of sorts."

"But it doesn't make sense, does it. If Rudy had used the syringe to somehow poison Joy, why would he keep the evidence?"

Maris watched as a car pulled up to the available pump. "And even if he did decide to keep it, how was he poisoned? By accident?" She shook her head. "You're right. It just doesn't hang together."

For a few moments there was silence. Then Mac said, "You have some news as well?"

"Not news, as such," she said, "but something I remembered about Rudy's office." She recounted the inventory data and wondered again if Superior Hardware might not be having cash flow problems. "In fact," she concluded, "Bear mentioned that they were still closed this morning."

"Oh?" Mac said. "I let Mrs. Schmid know yesterday that forensics was done."

"Hmm," they said together.

Maris heard a radio squawk in the background.

"If I come up with anything else," he said, "I'll give you a yell."

"Likewise," she said. "Thanks for the call."

"Anytime," he said, and hung up.

Just then, Guy Koch came out of the sandwich shop with a bag that looked very much like he'd ordered a couple of the subs.

Maris tucked the phone into her purse, grabbed the small stack of pizzeria coupons next to it, and got out of the car. But by the time she'd locked the door and turned to say hello, he'd gotten into a car on the far side of the station, at one of the pumps. She heard the engine start and knew he'd never hear her. As she watched him drive away, she wondered why the hardware store wasn't open.

As she started for the shop in order to make her request and pick up lunch, she wondered if maybe Rudy was the only person who actually knew how to run Superior Hardware.

31

To end her round of visits, Maris parked in front of Inklings New & Used Books. It'd be good to touch base with the Pages and see how they were doing. She shouldered her purse, entered the spacious store, and immediately found Alfred stocking books, and Minako behind the counter watering the lush wall of plants.

"Maris," Alfred said, setting the carton of books aside. "Two visits in one week. Aren't we the lucky ones?" Then he paused, his forehead furrowing as he stared at her. "Or are we?"

Maris smiled and held out her hand. "I am not the bearer of bad tidings, believe me." Alfred seemed to relax a little. "I stopped by to see how you two were doing."

Alfred laughed a little, though it sounded a bit forced. "A bit jumpy still, I guess." He ran his fingers through his light hair. "I understand there's been a second death."

As a customer mounted the staircase steps to the second floor, Minako came over and went to her husband's side. "Rudy Schmid?"

Alfred craned his neck to see the edge of the plaza through the bookstore's front display windows. "Superior Hardware is still closed."

Maris nodded. "Yes. I'm afraid so—and it was another case of botulism poisoning."

"Oh no," Minako said, and put a hand to her mouth.

"How dreadful," Alfred said, pulling her close.

"But I hasten to add," Maris said quickly, "that it doesn't look like an accident. In other words, I don't think there's any risk of people being accidentally poisoned."

"Or that it's just spreading somehow?" Minako asked.

Maris shook her head. "Absolutely not. It doesn't really work that way."

"Well," Alfred said, sounding tired. "We've only eaten at home since..."

"Picnic Day," Minako said quietly.

"Honestly," Alfred said. "We were feeling pretty lucky not to have had any of Joy's salsa."

Minako gave her husband a crooked half smile. "It wouldn't have gone with our bento lunches."

"Oh no," he agreed. "Of course not."

Maris recalled the bag of tortilla chips, the box of pizza, and the half-eaten tuna sandwich. "She brought her own lunch, a sandwich and chips, as I recall."

"Right," Alfred said.

"She wasn't much for cooking," Minako added.

"Oh?" Maris said. Perhaps putting together the ingredients for salsa wasn't quite considered 'cooking' but she'd at least gone to the trouble of making it.

Minako shook her head. "She never had time, with her teaching schedule at the school."

"So, she mostly ate out then?" Maris asked.

This time Alfred shook his head. "That was too expensive."

"And the restaurants in Cheeseman Village aren't as good as the ones here," Minako said.

Alfred shrugged a little. "Although that Mexican place is nice."

Minako crinkled her nose. "It's too spicy." She regarded Maris. "Joy thought so too."

Her husband gazed down at her. "You know, I'd forgotten that. That one time we went there, I liked their Salsa Colorado…"

"But Joy and I thought it was much too spicy," Minako finished.

"Hmm," Maris said. "Maybe that's why she made her own. She was on a budget and wanted it to be less spicy?"

For a moment the three of them looked at each other, until Minako and Alfred shrugged. "I don't know," they said.

Maris smiled at the two of them. "So you're eating at home and feeling well?"

"So far," Alfred said, his smile returning. "We take turns making lunch…"

"And dinner," Minako said. "It's been nice to spend more time in the kitchen."

Maris grinned at them. Of course they

took turns. She looked over to the cash register. "How is business?"

"Very good," Alfred said, indicating the carton he'd been emptying. "Maybe even a little better than usual."

"Really," Minako said, looking out the display windows, "it's the restaurants that might be more affected."

Maris had to nod. "I think you're right." She noticed the green, white, and red colored coupons for the pizzeria's opening on the counter next to the register. "Do you think you'll be going to Pizza del Popolo's grand opening?"

Minako's smile matched Alfred's as they both nodded. "We were planning on it," she said. "He's such a nice person."

Maris smiled back. "I agree." She adjusted the purse on her shoulder. "Then I'll let you get back to work, and see you there tomorrow night."

As Maris made her way back out onto the sidewalk, she paused and looked across the grass at the adjoining stretch of plaza. Through the pizzeria's window, she could see Max bustling about, near one of the ovens. Next door, however, a 'Closed' sign still hung in the window of Superior Hardware. Maris paused, frowning at the two stores.

Max was no doubt getting ready for his grand opening, but he must have one less customer these days, since Guy wasn't working next door. In fact, she'd just seen the pizzeria's best customer coming out of Flour Power with sub sandwiches.

The conversation with Mac while she'd been parked outside Jude and Fab's shop flashed through her mind: the hardware store's database and the obvious syringe. She glanced back over her shoulder. Joy thought the salsa at the Mexican restaurant was too spicy.

As a thought began to gel in her mind, Maris looked back at the hardware store's 'Closed' sign. The sheriff hadn't asked them to stay closed.

Quickly, she dug in her purse, yanked out her phone, and dialed Mac.

33

By the late afternoon, the sheriff had contacted and then assembled all of the interested parties at Superior Hardware. He and Maris had found the store's stock of folding chairs, as well as a few patio chairs and arranged them in a U-shape in the only space big enough to hold everyone—right in front of the door.

Maris stood at the open end of the horseshoe along with Mac.

"Thank you all for taking the time to come by," he said. "There have been a few developments in the recent botulism cases."

As always, Minako and Alfred sat together holding hands. Max sat next to them, followed around the top of the U by Guy and finally Heather, opposite Minako.

With a sad smile, Maris turned to the bookstore owners. "Joy Castro was not the target of a botulism poisoning."

Alfred's eyes got big behind his large glasses. Although his mouth dropped open a little, it was Minako who spoke. "But she died of botulinum toxin poisoning."

"You said so yourself," Alfred managed to add.

"Oh yes," Maris said. "Without a doubt that's what killed her." Maris glanced at Heather, but then looked back to Alfred. "After the argument at the picnic, we'd wondered if she'd been targeted."

Maris looked to Mac, who nodded. "After tracking down every last scrap of evidence, there is nothing to suggest that there was any connection between Rudy Schmid and Joy Castro. None at all."

"But," Alfred said, frowning, "if she wasn't the target..."

Minako gasped. "Are you saying it was us?" She turned a shocked expression to her husband, and then back to the sheriff.

"No," Mac assured them. "Neither of you was the target either."

Frowns deepened all around the circle.

Max raised his hand, as though he were in a classroom.

"Max," Maris said, "you have a question?"

"Those three sat together, eating," he said, likely voicing what the others were thinking. "On the same blanket. If Joy was not targeted, and the Pages were not targeted..."

"We'll come back to that," Mac said, causing Max to exchange a puzzled look with Alfred.

"Heather," Maris said to her.

The newly widowed woman grimaced a little. "I was wondering when you'd get around to me."

Maris crossed her arms in front of her. "And why would you be wondering that?"

Heather snorted. "Well I essentially admitted that the love had gone out of my marriage a long time ago, didn't I?" She didn't wait for an answer. "And I'm not a particularly good actress. There's no point in me trying to pretend that I'm distraught."

Maris dropped her arms. "It's not your marriage that interests me. It's your canning."

The woman blinked at her. "My what?"

Mac gestured toward her. "You've described your partnership with your deceased husband. While he worked and ran the store, you took care of the home."

"That's right," she said, regaining some of her calm. "I took care of the home and my husband. He took care of–"

"But the number one way to get botulism," Maris said, stopping her, "is from improperly canned food."

Heather scowled back at her. "Oh this is ridiculous." She glanced around the circle, only to find the others staring at her. "Look," she said, putting her hands flat on her thighs as though she was stabilizing herself. "I may not be the best cook or the most inventive canner out there, but I do know the rules." She leveled her gaze at Maris. "And I regularly eat my own canned food." She glanced at the sheriff. "And if there's some test or other that you want to do on me or my pantry, that's fine." She looked back to Maris. "I know how to can goods safely."

"I don't doubt it," Maris said to her, and pointedly turned to Max.

The Italian chef cocked his head back. "Me?" He put both hands over his heart. "You suspect me?" His flabbergasted look shot around the group. "But...but..." he sputtered and then groaned. "*No, mi amici, no.*"

Minako spoke up in the silence. "But I thought that his pizza from the picnic was tested and cleared?"

The sheriff hooked his thumbs behind the front of his utility belt. "Correct."

Max turned a grateful look on Minako. "Thank you," he said, bowing his head a little.

"Besides," Heather said, "why would a restauranteur start poisoning people with botulism when he's trying to get his restaurant going?"

Max looked at her as though it was his first time seeing her. "*Grazie, signora.*" He gazed around at the entire group and threw his hands up in the air. "I have said it from the start. My humble pizzeria has hardly started before it begins to sink."

Maris turned to Guy. "Despite support from your next-door neighbor here."

Guy smiled at her and then at Max. "You can't argue with good pizza."

"You know," Maris said to the hardware store employee, "I saw you at Flour Power today, picking up some subs. I tried to say hi but you'd already gotten in your car."

"Oh," he said, surprised. "I didn't see you."

"I know," she said simply. "But it got me wondering." She glanced at Minako and Alfred. "Joy was a teacher in Cheeseman Village and living by herself on a budget. You say she didn't eat out much."

Alfred and Minako nodded. "That's right," they said.

Maris turned back to Guy. "And yet Max says you've turned into his best customer. Then I see you at Flour Power. If I check with the smokehouse, would I find you patronize them as well?"

Guy shrugged his big shoulders. "I like good food just as much as the next person."

Maris nodded. "Naturally. But I wonder how you're able to afford it?" She glanced around at the hardware store. "I'm sure it's a nice place to work, but Rudy probably couldn't have afforded a lot in terms of a salary for a hardware clerk."

His smile slipped a little. "I get by." He glanced between her and Mac. "I don't know what you're trying to get at, but I owed Rudy my job." He nodded at Heather. "Your husband was the only person willing to take a chance on an ex-con."

"I wonder why the hardware store never seems to have enough stock on hand?" Maris said abruptly.

Guy glared at her. "What do you mean?"

"I bought the last box of medium nitrile gloves," she said and glanced at Max. "Bear had to improvise the fix on your oven when Superior Hardware didn't have the supplies he needed." She looked back to Guy. "When I discovered Rudy's body, you were with a customer who couldn't find what he wanted. In fact, more and more, Bear has to shop in Cheeseman Village."

Guy shrugged again. "I'm not in charge of ordering or the inventory."

"Ah," Maris said, holding up a finger. "That's right. The first morning that I visited, Rudy was out on the dock doing just that, taking an inventory. I would guess he found something amiss. The goods on hand didn't match the database—by a lot."

When Guy made no reply, the sheriff spoke up. "You'd have plenty of spending money if you were selling stolen goods, like pricey tools and supplies."

Maris watched Guy's jaw clench, and he seemed rooted to the folding chair. "Maybe it's not a love of good food that leads you to eat out so often. Maybe it's fear of your own kitchen." She paused, watching him. "You know. That place where you let the botulism bacteria grow." When he didn't react, she elaborated. "It's ridiculously easy to make if you know what you're doing, because the bacteria is everywhere."

"Had Mr. Schmid caught you stealing?" Mac asked him.

"Wait a minute," Heather said, shaking her head. "You're talking about murder. Over what? Some stolen tools?"

Mac shook his head slowly. "Not just over some stolen tools." He looked at Guy. "I've pulled your criminal record, Mr. Koch. You were incarcerated for selling pot, but you've also done time for assault and battery. Another conviction in this state means three strikes and you're out. You'd go back to prison for life." The sheriff touched the side of his own eye. "That scar of yours. Did you have a teardrop tattoo removed?"

Maris stared at the small spot.

Alfred glanced between the two men, and finally asked, "What's a teardrop tattoo?"

The sheriff never took his eyes from Guy. "In some prison cultures, it stands for a murder."

Though Guy said nothing, an ugly sneer twisted his upper lip.

Maris turned to the Pages. "There was no evidence of botulism found at Joy's home. Someone had to have given her the salsa." She looked at Guy. "To make up for the fact that she was thrown out of the store? Or simply as a gift, from a single man to a single woman?"

The ex-con's biceps were bulging and his neck took on a strained and stringy look.

Mac stepped forward. "Guy Koch, I'm placing you under arrest for the murders of Joy Castro and Rudy Schmid." The sheriff quickly removed the cuffs from his belt and took the ex-con by the arm. Guy's shoulders sagged and he bowed his head low as he stood. Maris had the brief impression this was something he'd been through many times. As Mac moved his wrists behind his back and put on the handcuffs, he said, "I've also obtained a search warrant for your apartment. If I'm not mistaken, we'll find not only botulism, but the items missing from the store's inventory." With one hand on the cuffs, and one on Guy's shoulder, he moved him toward the front door. "Let's go." Though the ex-con shuffled, he didn't resist.

Mac gave Maris a small nod as they passed her, and then they were gone. She could hear his voice fading as he read Guy his rights.

"But," Minako said, standing. "I don't understand about Joy. She didn't have anything to do with this store, let alone the stealing."

"It's true," Maris said to her, as the others also stood. "Guy didn't target Joy—or anyone for that matter. He simply wanted someone else to die of botulism. She was simply a distraction, meant to create confusion."

"*Che disgustozo*," Max muttered, his face screwed up as though he'd tasted something awful. "That's disgusting."

"So any one of us could have died?" Alfred asked.

Maris nodded. "I'm afraid so. I don't think Guy was picky."

As the group slowly filed out, Maris

thought back on Mojo's Ouija clue. Guy had served time for assault and 'battery.' The man on the tarot card had certainly looked like he'd gotten away with something—not just theft but murder as well. When Heather hung back, Maris stopped just outside the shop's door and turned back to her.

Heather held up a set of keys. "I'm just going to lock up."

34

The big day had arrived, and Maris found she was excited. Using a hand truck, she wheeled her heavy box along the Towne Plaza's sidewalk. Cookie strode alongside her, a potted plant with a luxurious bunch of herbs in her hand, and a serving tray under her other arm. The evening had turned pleasantly cool and the last violet rays of the dramatic sunset were giving way to a Prussian blue.

"Beautiful night for a grand opening," Cookie said.

"I couldn't agree more," Maris said. "I've really been looking forward to this."

But even from a few stores away, Maris could see that there was hardly anyone in the vicinity.

"Wait," Cookie said. "What's this?"

Maris realized she was walking alone, stopped, and looked behind her. The diminutive chef was looking up at something. A temporary vinyl sign was hung over the hardware store's real sign.

"Heather's Hardware," Cookie read. She turned to Maris and smiled. "Interesting."

Maris grinned back. "Interesting indeed."

But they didn't have to wait long to get some answers. The only person in the pizzeria was Heather Schmid. When Max saw them, he threw his arms open wide.

"*Mi amici*," he said, giving Maris an air kiss on each cheek. "My friends," he said to Cookie doing the same. "Welcome and thank you for coming."

"We wouldn't have missed it, Chef," Cookie said to him and handed him the pot. "Some oregano from our garden."

"Oh," he gushed. Then he pinched his fingers together, and made a show of kissing them. "Fresh herbs. Nothing is better. Nothing." He bowed to her. "Thank you."

"Heather," Maris said to her. "I see there are some changes taking place at the hardware store."

She lifted her hands with a shy smile. "It's my only source of income. I'm going to see if I can turn it around."

"Maybe start a new chapter in your life," Maris said smiling. "I can highly recommend it."

Heather glanced at the hand truck and box. "What have you got there?"

Maris stooped down and opened the box. Max was just returning from setting the oregano in the front window when she pulled out one of the bottles of wine and a corkscrew.

"Complimentary wine," the B&B owner said. She set them down on the shelf table to the side. Then she took out the plastic cups. "Courtesy of the Pixie Point Bay Lighthouse."

Max blinked at her, then the wine, then back at her. "I am astonished," he gasped. Then he held out a hand. "Not at your generosity, *Bella*, but what about your guests?"

She gave him a sly smile. "They're just parking."

As she opened the first bottle, Cookie said, "Oh, there they are."

Patricia and the Yangs seemed to be chatting as they approached, all of them holding the tri-colored coupons. Maris greeted them with cups of wine on the serving tray. "Good to see you."

Although the Yangs paused to each take a cup, the food critic proceeded directly to the man in the chef's uniform. "This smells positively divine." As she fell into an animated conversation about the menu, Maris caught Cookie's eye.

"It's getting a little crowded in here." She nodded to the door. "Shall we?"

Mac was the next to arrive, carrying the small folding table that Maris had requested. He was looking particularly dashing in the black evening jacket, matching trousers, and crisp white dress shirt. "Table for two?" he said, smiling at her.

"Sounds perfect," she said, grinning back at him. Once it was set up, she put the tray of wine cups down on it. "Help me get the wine?"

In another few minutes, the wine box was on the sidewalk outside, with the table and tray.

"The forensics crew should be here any minute," he said.

Maris stopped pouring and looked up at him. "Forensics?"

He chuckled a little as he set down the empty plastic cups. "For good eats."

Cookie chuckled, and Maris sighed with relief. "Good," she finally said. "Good."

"Is that Jude and Fabiola?" Cookie asked. "What is that they're carrying?"

They were crossing the plaza from the direction of the Oriental gazebo, and walking too far apart. But then Maris saw that they held something strung between them. Only when they reached the sidewalk did Maris see what it was—a string of little paper lights. Jude had a coiled extension cord slung over his shoulder.

"Oh goodness, you two," Maris said to them. "What a great idea."

Fab flashed her gorgeous model smile at her. "It's not a party without party lights."

Jude took off the extension cord, glancing at the pizzeria. "Then let's get it started." He sniffed the air. "Wow, that smells great." He exchanged a look with his wife. "Let's hurry."

The growing group on the sidewalk attracted a couple who seemed hesitant but interested. Maris took the tray of wine over to them.

"Welcome to Pizza del Popolo's grand opening," she said. "Complimentary wine on the house."

"Oh, thank you," the woman said.

As the man took a glass as well, Maris regarded the brightly lit restaurant and nodded to it. "So far, the Calzone Vesuvio is my favorite. It comes with all the toppings you'd expect—and some wonderful ones you don't. Well worth a try."

"Thanks," the man said, as he and his companion made their way to the restaurant.

"Maris," said a familiar voice. "Are you serving wine?"

She turned to see Delia and Eugene Burnside approaching. Both were carrying a stack of white plates.

"Aren't your customers going to need those?" Maris asked, smiling.

"Of course," Delia said, "and they're right behind us. We've decided to close for the evening."

As they passed, Eugene winked at her. "Keep your pepper dry, young lady." Then his head snapped toward the pizzeria. "My that smells enticing." The two of them waded through the growing crowd.

Mac brought more cups and had opened another bottle of wine. As he poured, the street lamps came up, bathing the surroundings in a beautiful glow. But when the Toussaint's party lights went on, draped between the restaurant and the nearest lamp, there was a murmur of appreciation—followed by the noise of the crowd ratcheting up a notch.

Someone touched Maris on the shoulder and she turned to find the owner of Plateau 7.

"*Bonsoir*," he said to her.

"Etienne," she said. "Thank you so much for coming."

He eyed the crowd in the pizzeria. "I think I have arrived just in time," he said, hardly pausing. "Let me see what I can do."

As the event grew larger, it attracted more people—just as Maris had hoped. As she and Mac circulated with the wine, people were eating and laughing, and simply having a good time. Lucille and Sefina were in the growing crowd, as were Alfred and Minako. She hadn't seen any of them arrive. But everyone that she had called on for help had delivered above and beyond.

"Speech," someone called out. "Chef Cuore! Speech!"

More calls for Max sounded, and finally he emerged from the restaurant. The crowd immediately burst into applause and there were shouts of "Bravo!".

Max clasped his hands together over his head, shaking them, and then over his heart. When his gaze landed on Maris, he quickly waved at the crowd for quiet.

"Speech," someone yelled. Someone else answered, "Let him speak!"

As quiet slowly spread, Max lowered his hands, and someone handed him a cup of wine. He held it to his heart as he looked around him, grinning madly.

"*Mi amici*," he started, then shook his head. "No." He gazed around looking at each of them, and even from the edge of the crowd, Maris could see that he was misty-eyed. "*Mi familia*. How truly, truly lucky I am. I...I don't know what to say." He held out his plastic cup. "Except...*grazie mille*. Thank you. A thousand times over, thank you. This..." His voice broke a little. "...would not have been possible without you." He looked directly at Maris, his eyes gleaming. Then he raised his wine high in the air. "To Pixie Point Bay."

As the crowd answered with a hearty and loud reply, Maris and Mac smiled and lifted their cups as well. "To Pixie Point Bay."

DEDICATION

For Mr. Bee's Knees

COPYRIGHT

Copyright © 2020 Emma Belmont

www.ingramcontent.com/pod-product-compliance
Lightning Source LLC
Chambersburg PA
CBHW050518190726

48284CB00003B/860